B O R D E R S II (NORTH EAST)

AN EXTENEDED PART OF B O R D E R S ALREADY PUBLISHED BY THIS AUTHOR ON PENCIL PLATFORM

BY

MD ANOWAR ISLAM

ISBN 978-93-5458-025-3

Published in India 2021 by Pencil

A brand of
One Point Six Technologies Pvt. Ltd.
123, Building J2, Shram Seva Premises,
Wadala Truck Terminal, Wadala (E)
Mumbai 400037, Maharashtra, INDIA
E connect@thepencilapp.com
W www.thepencilapp.com

Author biography

Born of a middle class family, the author, Md. Anowar Islam is a lawyer and journalist by profession and passed his Matriculate examination from S. Ali Govt. Aided High School, Sukchar (Assam in 1977 and completed his Arts Graduation from Tura Govt. College (Meghalaya in 1981. He pursued his higher studies in law in J.B. Law College, Guwahati and obtained LL.B degree from there subsequently and completed Master Degree in Arts from Gauhati University thereafter in 1990. He also passed the NCTVT training course in stenography from Tura ITI, Tura earlier. He entered government service early in 1981 and served various departments both under State mad Central Governments at Guwahati, Goalpara and Tura. He also served as Lecturer in Goalpara Law College for sometime, as also in Kazi & Zaman College, New Bhaitbari and then in Hatsingimari College. He joined the Tura Bar Association sometime in 1992. His journalistic works started practically as back as in 1979 immediately after successfully participating in the Competition Success Review Essay Contest No.293 and has by now composed a large number of poems in English, Assamese, Bengalee and Hindi as well. He has also established a good rapport as an outstanding educationist, author, writer of note books and poet and has had a lot of published works done and contributed to different dailies of the North Eastern Region and joined as an active mofussil newspaper reporter sometime in 1991 and associated himself with The Assam Tribune, The North-

East Times, The Meghalaya Guardian, The Shillong Times and as a freelancer to The Telegraphs etc. and so on so forth. His poetic compositions have come to be published in different local books and magazines while his efforts to publish a local BI-lingual weekly, Sapta-Dhwani from Hatsingimari (Assam) from February, 2000 as the founder editor, although could not be successfully carried through, yet brought him acclamation from all corners. He has associated with different social organizations and served as Members and Advisers in different organizations like the Meghalaya Board of Wakfs, Assam Unnati Sabha, Animal Welfare Board of India, Total Literacy Campaign, West Garo Hills district, Meghalaya, Founder President of Hatsingimari Press Club and so on. He has also been honoured with Rashtriya Rattan Award in 2004 , followed by an Award given away by a Dhubri-based local weekly publications group. He has been a great social activist rendering social services all through his life in association with Red-Cross Society and many other local NGOs and will continue to serve the people as such in all future to come. At present he is practicing as an Advocate under Hatsingimari Bar Association, and holding a key position of Headman in his own eleca with sufficient pull over the mass people

Author.

Contents

Chapter – III

Chapter – III

North-East

Indigenous Versus Immigrants in North-East

Be it the Bengali Hindus, the Muslim peasantry, the Nepalees, the tea-garden labourers from Chotanagpur or he repatriates of erstwhile East Pakistan, the genesis of reigners' influx is, indeed, in most cases drawn right back he the British time, which, unfortunately, fails to include those who had entered into and settled down in the - East by virtue of their mighty invasions prior to the of the British colonial government

hile, the word "immigrant" as an antonym to us" appears to have become most common in use circles as a necessary substitute for "foreigner" prefixable to qualify a noun than a noun in itself, viz, immigrant Muslims, immigrant Nepalees, immigrant Hindus and so on. However, before we step in on and dive deep into the subject, it may be expedient to know what exactly the word "immigrant" stands for, and how far one tends to use it correctly or incorrectly with particular reference to "indigenous" and migration, settlement or resettlement of different people, which took place in the distant or nears past in this part of India.

According to various Dictionaries, the word "immigration" as a noun means migration of a person from one country to another, not as a mere tourist or visitor but as a settler. However, in order to know the exact/actual implication and correctness of the word "immigrant" in the present context one needs to have a nostalgic assessment and objective review of our past history first.

As borne out by history, consequent on the Burmese depredations and the toughest economic crisis that followed in Assam owing to acres of lands remaining pasture and ever uncultivated, the British Government, who had just taken over the legacy of administration of this region had to inflate the land with a huge number of Bengali settlers belonging to both Hindu and Muslim peasantry from the adjacent province of Bengal, and thereby encouraged increased agricultural activities and trades in order to recapitulate the economic status and make public life happier.

It may, however, be mentioned here that the new Bengali settlers were not at all happy with this inter-provincial migration, and on the contrary they demonstrated their passive resentment over the exorbitant and higher revenues exacted by the Zamindars, which again caused their frequently migrating from place to place within the province of Assam.

This migratory trend had, at one stage, assumed so alarming a proportion that it posed a serious threat to the economic stability of the region once again, and the government had to further adopt the policy of granting revenue-free homestead, garden lands etc. to attract these settlers. In this context, it is pertinent to also mention that the system of land survey and issue of leases was enforced keeping this very damaging factor in view, and more so not to allow any further migration of these people.

Likewise, the Bengal traders, mostly belonging to Bengali Hindus and other Europeans, who along with the Muslim peasantry having permanently settled down in Assam, completely assimilated with the Assamese culture except in Surma Valley and Goalpara district in BrahmaputraValley, where the Bengal culture still persisted to dominate due to historical reasons.

Needless to say, during the British rule, the whole of India, including Bangladesh and Pakistan had constituted into a single country and the constituent provinces and other princely states being tributary at best to the British government, commanded no status of a separate country to treat the inter-provincial migration of a people as amounting to "immigration".

As a matter of comparison and better understanding, the logic as put forward in the foregoing paragraphs is as straight and genuinely effective as to the migration of a "Tamil" from Tamil Nadu, as provided in our Constitution, and taking to settle down, say, in Assam. The two being the constituent states only of free India, such a migration is in no way be construed as constituting "immigration" nor can the "Tamil" be called an "immigrant" in the state of Assam.

Be that as it may, it may be recalled that in this unique land of different plains and hills tribesmen including such other aboriginal ethnic groups like the Bodos, the Kacharis, the Khasis, the Jaintias, the Garos and so forth, there has taken place a great sea-change over the centuries in terms of population structure and social reconstruction consequent on repeated invasions and depredations, entry and settlement of a huge number of foreign powers and other foreign settlers, be they the Pathans, the Mughals, the Ahoms or others.

While speaking about foreign invasions, one finds a striking synchronization between the entries of the Mohammedans and the Ahoms into the North East. It may be noted that the Pathans had first invaded Assam from the west early 1206 AD and was followed by the Mughals, while the Ahoms entered this province in 1228 AD through Patkai ranges on the extreme northeast. Both the groups of people ruled the land to a limited scale, the Muslims having ruled down Kamrup district, the Ahoms up Kamrup district.

Nevertheless, their ruling the land does not necessarily indemnify them (Muslims and Ahoms both) from the depredations they caused to the aboriginals in alienating their age-old traditional cultural identity and social status including their life-style. Nor does it legalise their entry, if it is deemed to be illegal at all in a wider perspective, and thereby make them or confer on them both the undisputable status of being called as "indigenous people" of Assam.

Contrarily, if the Bengal people, who were but the citizens of the then united India, could be called as "immigrant" in the then Assam there is no logic then to exclude the Ahoms and the Pathans or the Mughals, who were all but the foreigners in this land, from being equally called as "immigrants" or in similar terminology.

It goes without saying, India, after she became free in 1947, went through a great vicissitude, and was partitioned into two separate nations, viz, Hindustan and Pakistan. Meanwhile, as victims of the unfortunate partition, people those who were repatriated from the erstwhile West Pakistan had unquestionably come to be known as "repatriates" in India. But how far the "repatriates" of the then East Pakistan (now Bangladesh) could retain this status in the North-East is a matter which may call for a detailed scrutiny, owing to their having blended with the original Bengal settlers and other Bengali Infiltrators, who might have crossed over to India illegally and settled down in this region at a later stage.

Thus, the mess created by the three different groups of Bengali Hindu settlers owing to their ethnic and linguistic affinity has given rise to their being miscategorised as“immigrant” with no palpable distinction in the eyes of a section of the people.

Similarly, the Bengali Muslim peasantry, who came over to this part of India and settled down in the North-Eastern areas will back in British time, cannot also easily be distinguished and singled out from those who might have illegally intruded into this country after Independence, owing to an identical ethnic and linguistic including religious affinity they maintain. Accordingly, they are also much prone to come under the category of “immigrants” regardless of their allegience and citizenship to the country. This is their sad predicament which can be obviated but seems not to be a soft nut to crack at all.

The case with the Nepalees is also no better and different from the predicament the Bengali Muslims and Hindus, hitherto brought into this country or repatriated, suffer from. As regards the tea-garden labourers brought mostly from Chotanagpur, their status does not seem to have been least affected or jeopardized by any degree uptil this date except for making references here and references there sometime or the other.

It is, therefore, obviously cloud-stained, barring the aboriginals and such other ethnic groups, whom to call “indigenous” and who not given the fact that under the process of linguistic transformation and cultural fusion, there has emerged a neo-culture known as “Assamese Culture” in Assam through the centuries. One wishes that this very cultural fusion and synthesis be not got lost sight of while deciding the question of one’s identity and citizenship to the extent required for justices' sake and fair play.

(Filed to newspapers by A. Islam in August 26,1988)

Historical Boundaries in North-East

But in an isolated manner, much has been talked, discussed, debated and deliberated at various level including the Press about what is called the "Controversial Boundary Disputes" between Assam and her neighbouring sister-states, viz, Meghalaya, Nagaland, Arunachal Pradesh etc. ever since the latter came into being. Yet nothing formally acceptable by all concerned could be evolved to resolve the longstanding issue once for and all.

Even the repeatedly talked about reports like that of Chandrachud Commission set up to enquire into various aspects and justification, if any of the claims and counter-claims, as also a series of meetings of the concerned Chief Ministers etc. held in this regard could hardly bring any tangible results towards solution to this problem.

This is partly because, so far my personal feelings go, nobody in the helm of the concerned State affairs desires to be unnecessarily dragged into the issue and get maligned for parting with any portion of their respective State territory, and partly because they all want the issue to be kept ever alive as an advantageous means to gain political mileage, as also to avoid any adverse attribution tantamount to damaging the image of their respective government in the State.

Further, the Centre is always seen to be in search of some opportunities to score points in its insatiable bid for gaining political advantages over non-Congress (I) governments through guided instrumentality of the States run by its own party governments. The Centre's casual attitude and marked indifference on this score again is nothing but a perceptible exercise to build its party image in the state level, which though may not force Assam to concede to the claims of her sister-states yet may overshadow the AGP credibility towards protecting their own people from the miscreants operating in the inter-state border areas who are patronized by the neighbouring Congress (I)-run state governments themselves.

The inter-state boundary dispute is indeed a good source of striking at public sentiment. Thus, while the AGP government does not display itself to be too smart and overactive to welcome public wrath in this regard by way of any concession to the claims staked by its sister-states, the Centre on the other hand, and contrary to public expectations is seen to indirectly fuel and involve itself in such of those unfortunate incidents as that of Rajapukhuri occurred in a recent past on the Assam-Nagaland border and so on. It may be mentioned that the Rajapukhuri incident claimed a lot of innocent lives leading to the signing of the Mahanta-Jamir Agreement for, inter-alia, restraining any further incident of such a heinous nature.

It is therefore high time that all the political parties and their governments involved here shunned their respective rigid stands and put their heads together in order to review the issue covering the entire North-East on a far broader perspective and some concrete ways and means evolved to end this contentious issue once for and all. This has become quite imperative today to prevent any further loss of innocent lives, and more so because the Mahanta-Jamir Agreement-like agreement and certain routine talks and discussions alone will not suffice to control further deterioration of the situation. In fact, it requires still concreter a plan to be thought about and given a reasonable shape as well. In this context, a few points as noted below may be given a due thought and consideration:

1)

The entire gamut of inter-state boundary

disputes in the North-East as a whole may be viewed as a single national problem without any room left for deviation and gaining any political advantage or imposing disadvantages;

1)

The Centre should take some positive steps to resolve the problem, and should not use it only as a political bandwagon and vehicle of scoring points in its favour;

2)

It may indeed be appreciably borne in mind that every

miniature event of the past, recent and remote both, is a component of our history. Each of such event is, however, limited to itself in terms of time and extent because, as for an example the following cases of historical events speaks volumes about it:

a)

Messers Kelso and Bedford earlier during British administration demarcated the northern boundary of Garo Hills district;

b)

This was, however, revised later on by Mr. Backett, who drew the boundary line far beyond that of Kelso-Bedford covering a considerable portion of the then Goalpara district;

c)

The second event led to an irresistible border dispute, which had, however, culminated in recognizing the Kelso-Bedford line as the boundary in fact between Goalpara (Assam) and Garo Hills (Meghalaya) and that of Mr. Backett in effect. This is so because an arrangement was made under which the land falling in between the two (Kelso-Bedford and Backett) lines was recognized to belong to the Goalpara Zamindars but was to be administered by the Deputy Commissioner, Garo Hills, while The revenue collected were to be paid to the Goalpara Zamindars and so paid too till before abolition of Zamindari System in Assam;

d)

Thus, in the spirit of the third event, though the Zamindari system is no longer in vogue, the lands falling within the said two lines still belong to Goalpara district (Old) but for being limited to be part of Garo Hills district by time and event. Who knows there will occur not yet another event to bypass the earlier events? In that case which one is to be insisted on ? Perhaps none but the current one, and/or at best the one which takes auto-formation overlooking all time-bound barrages, and not because history says so and so. The British didn't bother what the Mughal did but the one they could do and thereby created new history. Can't we do what we think best fitted to our time ?

3)

The claims and counter-claims in regard to the disputes in question seem to be partially based on the boundaries drawn by the British government and partially not. This can, however, not be the only basis of settling the disputes. Can Assam claim and get, confining the matter within its own history, the original territory of ancient Kamrupa only because it had once flourished, without, however, any duly demarcated boundaries, over a large 74

tract of territory presently falling under Bangladesh, West Bengal, Bihar etc. ? Perhaps not, because of being limited by time and extent. If not, now can then the crisis in question be favoured only on historical grounds ?

4)

Apart from the claims and counter-claims already put foreward by the interested groups, there may be yet some more such areas, namely, the entire plain portion of Garo Hills district of Meghalaya etc., where people, having all ethnic and linguistic affinity with those of the neighbouring state, are living only under obligation of boundary and not because they cherish living in such a State. In fact, these people may be far more deprived as compared to their kith and kin living in the neighbouring state in all material sense either because of various constitutionally authorized discriminatory policies of reservation, trade barriers and/or so, or because the concerned governments are not looking into their problems, rights and liberties as required under the mandate of the Constitution;

5)

In the event of a final settlement of the boundary disputes, such of those areas as facing similar problems need also to be identified by a suitably set-up authority by calling for memorandum/representation from the interested groups along with the disputed ones in order to gauge their sentiment and aspirations and value them too accordingly;

6)

Alternatively, a referendum, which may not be outside the purview of our Constitution, if conducted in respect of all the disputed and such of those identified areas as may be ascertained by the appropriate authority, would, to my personal estimation, go a long way in permanently resolving the boundary disputes in the entire North-East.

In any case, it is the common people only who matter most in arriving at an appropriate decision as to whether they will or will not be happy to live under the territorial jurisdiction of particular state. This must not be done or imposed upon by the elite group because their ideas and attitude are always tinged with the game of politics and exploitation of public sentiment.

Let the livers themselves decide whether to merge or not to merge their places of habitation with any of the states of the Union of India where they feel their interests will be best served and safeguarded. It should invariably be left on their own verdict to choose between the two options and settle the problem democratically.

(Authored by A. Islam during AGP rule in Assam)

o0o

Chapter-V

Meghalaya & Assam

Whither Non-Tribal Legislators of Meghalaya

Although belated, reports from various sections of the press indicate of a positive Government stand in re-assuring itself towards maintaining law and order etc. at the fake end of its taciturn role of a helpless spectator, purportedly, following the directives of the Prime Minister, Rajiv Gandhi to Capt. Sangma as a consequence of the threat of the five Congress (I) non-tribal MLAs to resign in protest against the leadership's lukewarm attitude towards protecting the life, property and interests of the non-tribal citizens permanently living in Meghalaya. In view of the continuing violence and regular curfew under Phulbari Police Station of Garo Hills district etc., however, such an indication is belied in too.

All is said and done. What has been done cannot perhaps be undone now. It is, however, quite fabulous to note that these non-tribal legislators, who had more trust on Capt. Sangma's unflattered leaderships than perhaps even on God, had all along bungled and cheated their people with sheer lies, and eventually their falsehood encompassed with the leadership's subterfuge assurances of adequate protection to the non-tribals, more than six unreserved Assembly seats etc. proved unavailing, and thus the aggrieved legislators, only at the eleventh hour, have taken up to raise hue and cry against the injustices meted out on the non-tribals.But how far they command peoples' trust is yet to be seen since, even during the first few months of the present violence too, they did not still cease to remain complacent and keep quiet. The invigorated gesture of their being finally brought home of the folly of remaining inept and passing time in complete hibernation is undoubtedly a welcome sign.

Still then as reportedly admitted and alluded to in their letter, addressed to the Chief Minister, Capt. W.A. Sangma and presently under consideration of the Political Affairs Committee(PAC), by the nontribal legislators themselves, "during the last ten years not a single nontribal was employed in Meghalaya Civil Service, ... total ban on land transfer even from a nontribal to a nontribal has gradually snatched away whatever little land resources they had. This particular aspect of the legislation is illegal and unconstitutional", one is very much inclined to know where did these learned legislators have been in those crucial moments during which such a legislation was debated and enacted on the floor of the Assembly ? It is also a moot point, should they be ready once again to sacrifice even contesting the elections as very dramatically demanded of the by a similar but counter-letter addressed to the PAC by the four tribal legislators (all Ministers) with various other imputations for ensuring Congress (I) majority etc. vis-à-vis the letter issued by the nontribal legislators. This party syndrome is most likely to prove now very fatal to them either.

So far as my little knowledge reaches, almost all the present nontribal legislators including late Capt. Manik Das, late Mozibur Rahman and Alhaj Akramuzzaman (now reportedly living in South Salmara, Assam following violences at Phulbari) and others were all holding the memberships of the Assembly during the course of this particular piece of legislation banning land transfer. But unfettered tributes must go to late Rahman, the iron man, who had alone gathered the requisite courage to vehemently oppose and raise strong objection and finally staged a historic walk out against this preposterous legislation, while all other members present then simply stuck to the party (Congress-I) principle and kept cryptic silence pretending ignorance of the very nature of its precarious implication for which they are now only crying wolf ? Late Rahman must be lamenting in the grave at the sort plight of these poor-sighted legislators.

Alas! What a superb judiciousness do bear our beloved learned legislators in axing their own legs only to subsequently cry wolf for healing, upon whom relies the very nature of the lass of the land, asprirations of the citizens and future prosperity of the nation. Can India bear the burden of such dumpish legislators, who can see their people being beheaded and perish before their own eyes, due to the thinly veiled party syndrome and apprehension of being an outcaste even after 40 glorious years of her political freedom and Constitutional Democracy ? Let us see how bold our legislators are to facae the new challenge of party syndrome.

(Filed to newspapers on the wake of violence and reservation of Assembly seats in Meghalaya during 1987-88)

o0o

Living a life Other than Tribals in Meghalaya

It is no denying the fact that our Constitution provided for certain safeguards to the Scheduled Castes, Scheduled Tribes and other backward classes of people with the noble object to bring them up to the national mainstream. Originally these safeguards including administrative autonomy guaranteed under the Sixth Schedule to the Constitution were envisaged only for a period of ten years from the date of commencement of the Constitution, the term has, however, been subsequently extended every ten years through constitutional amendments effected on ground of necessity for further development of these people. Presumably, the present term which expires in 1990, also is likely to be extended by a further period of ten years and may continue to be so extended by yet another few more such terms.

Meanwhile, there have been many other occasions when constitutional amendments including other legislations were also brought into effect at different stages of time in regard to protection of tribal interests and as a result, besides other safeguards, some of the tribal autonomous districts emerged into full-fledged States under different Acts of Parliament. Meghalaya, one of these new States --- tiny both in geographical size and population --- created with the two autonomous district of Garo Hills and Khasi-Jaintia Hills, continues to run under dual administration. Dual in the sense that the autonomous District Councils exercise certain autonomy in some areas of administration while the State Government is responsible for administration of the entire State.

The State is dominated by Garo, Khasi and Jaintia people, all recognized as Scheduled Tribes, and only about

4 lakhs, out of a total of about 15 lakhs population, are covered by nontribals comprising of Hindus, Muslims, Nepalees and some other plains tribes, viz, Koch, Rabha, Bodo, Kachari etc., who have only recaently been recognized as Scheduled Tribes as well in Meghalaya. And besides the Capital town, Shillong, a vast plain belt lying the district of Garo Hills including Tura town, is however, dominated by non-tribals comprising of Hindus and Muslims both.

Be that as it may, the real fact is that Meghalaya is a Hill State where, other constraints apart, nontribals as a whole enjoy little rights and the very basic constitutional rights of these people stand almost abridged under different Acts and laws of the State Legislature and District Councils respectively. The Meghalaya Transfer of Land (Regulation) Act, the Maintenance of Public Order Ordinance and various District Councils (trading by nontribals) Acts. Etc. are some of the enacatments which have put nontribal citizens in great disadvantage either on their legally settled lands, inheritence, movement, education, employment and trades including other profession for earning their bare livelihood also.

Ironically enough, the Meghalaya Transfer of Land (Regulation) Act which imposes an unreasonable restriction on acquisition and disposal including inheritance of lands even amongst the nontribals itself appears to be in contravention of the provisions of the Constitution of India, which envisages imposition on tribal people only to protecat their interests in lands and not on the nontribals at all, and hence it is ultra-vires the Constitution.

The 58th Constitution (Amendment) Act which received the assent of thePresident just sometime back amending Article 332 (3), providing for 55 reserved out of 60 Assembly seats in Meghalaya leaving only 5 general seats for the nontribals, where again a tribal candidate can also contest election, deprived the nontribal people of an adequate representation in the State Assembly. This ensues that nontribals permanently living in this State shall now enjoy only half the franchise and citizenship and not in full.

It may perhaps be the most unfortunate and isolated an event in our democracy and constitutional history of India that while one set of citizens shall enjoy full democracy the other (nontribals) set cannot even send any representative from their own community either to the State Assembly or to the Parliament. When the very right to franchise (to vote or to be voted) is halved against all establaished principles of democracy where does then stand the status of these poor people as citizens of India? A citizen minus the right to franchise falls in the same footing as the foreigners because only a foreigner, under the Constitution, can enjoy no political right or right to franchise in India.

It has been observed during the past few months that in the guise of foreigners' problems the State of Meghalaya is being gradually put into the throes of communal passions. The systematic attack on Nepalee-speaking people, loot and destrucation of their properties by the hooligans in Shillong followed by the inhuman torture on the nontribals (Hindus, Muslims etc.) at Tura and other parts including plain areas of Garo Hills district indicate that the anti-social elements are rampant in otherwise peaceful Meghalaya and their violent activities have marred the entire administration with a paralytical effect on normal life.

This presupposes that the basis under which the issue of foreigners is gaining greater momentum in Meghalaya day by day is nothing other than the shooting up of the State population from a bare 10 lakhs to 15 lakhs during the decade preceding 1981 Census. This quantum jump in population is, no doubt, one of the factors contributing to the idea and feeling of foreigners' influx and consequent apprehension of the indigenous people being swamped in the State.

However, as is generally attaributed, it may not be a true evaluation of facts that only the Bangladeshi Muslims or Hindus including Nepalees from Nepal do cross over to India and along with other outsiders find a heaven to settle down in Meghalaya. There appears to be a huge number of Garo refugees and such other infiltrators, who under the direct patronage of some Garo leaders came over to India from across the border during 1962 alone and settled down in various parts of Garo Hills district. This undesired trend of Garo influx continued even after the Bangladesh

Liberation War in 1971 also leading to a substantial increase in Garo population in the State.

One of the major and most appalling causes of population explosion in Meghalaya is the abnormally higher growth and birth rate amongst the Muslim gentry and some other plains tribes. These peculiarities aside, entry of somne amount of outsiders in the shape of daily labourers, wage-earners and petty businessmen including other foreign infiltrators may also be the other factors contributing to the seemingly high explosion of population and consequent foreigners' problem. The agitation launched by the Khasi Students Union in this regard leaving aside the Garos to sleep and snore, if not at best to counter it, itself, however, lightens the weightage and genuineness of such attribution of nontribal influx in so far as it commands support of the Khasi sentiment only.

Incidentally, the Khasi Students' Union including Congress (I) MP, Prof. G.G. Swell's campaign for a Khasi Chief Minister in preference to a Garo one seems to be an outcome of brewing up of a feeling amongst the Khasis that increase in Garo population alone by way of Garo influx is most likely to outnumber the Khasis and perpetuate Garo Chief Ministerhip by virtue of Garo-Nongaro joint support to Capt. W.A.Sangma's ruling party.

In the meantime, the sense of Garo-Khasi disparagement started generating some anti-Garo feeling in Khasi Hills district and the incident at Tura was perhaps only an exercise to prevent this mushroom growth of anti-Garo sentiment, first by fanning out tension through spread of mischievous rumours and then exploiting the situation by engineering communal riots under the direct patronage of some politicians belonging to the ruling party. This had probably necessitated a high level conspiracy --- as is evident from the circulation of cyclostyled copies of the alleged letter dispatched by one, Sahil Hussain, addressed to the Principal, Tura Govt. College making some derogatory remarks against the Garo community as a whole only to spread communal tension --- in order to protect the tribal solidarity as well in Meghalaya.

Khasis, who are the majority population, appear to be more concerned on the galloping increase in the State population than the Garos because of a straight decline in their own population. This is apparent from the concern and categorical statement of some of the Khasi leaders that "Small Family Norms is Not Acceptable in Meghalaya" and the whole gamut of the KSU movement seems to be politically motivated and is the handiwork of a section of these leaders including Prof. Swell only to bring about a political crisis and dillusion of the elecatorate towards the ruling Congress (I) party with an eye to gain ground in the ensuing election scheduled for February next in the state.

Unfortunately, however, Capt. Sangma, who felt much disturbed and discomfort over these undesirable developments, himself fell victims of this political mismanoeuvering and exploitation of Khasi sentiment by the Khasi and other Opposition leaders, and as a result a genuine crisis of saving his own political career and Congress (I) image in the State came before him compelling him to meet almost all the demands of the KSU including pleading for adequate reservation of Assembly seats and offering himself to resign if the Centre declined to extend Inner-Line Regulation to Meghalaya at the cost of nontribal interests. Not only that he had gone against the nontribal interests alone to please KSU and contain the carisis but he had gone much ahead to deprive his own Garo community also by reducing the percentage of their share in Govt. jobs to 33% from 40% as per the new Job Reservation Policy of the government.

Thus the real crisis which plagues the State today appears to be more for powers than for the serious economic and other relative pitfalls that worry the common masses most. Outward concerns, which is the core of all political exploitation, as shown by some politicians and other vested interests, utilized more as tool for exploiting public sentiment than for protecting their various interests, and all central aids etc. being eaten up by the corrupt practices of the higher-ups in the government, have added more to the present problems in the State than ever before.

There are indeed some genuine problems which calls for an early solution. Nevertheless, the manner in which political mismanoeuvring is fast breeding and the anti-socials are gaining totality on normal social life does not seem to be conducive either to the State or national interests. Our politicians should own some responsibility and irrespective of their party affiliations try more to ensure that the common people are not cowed down in the process of any political game. It should also be ensured that the prevailing atmosphere of brotherhood and the sense of peaceful co-existence for a harmonious development of the state is jeopardized no longer which may prove yet more disastrous to us all.

(Filed to newspapers by A. Islam on November 26,1987)

o0o

Development of Minorities in Meghalaya

Newspapers reports indicate that based on the disturbing findings of the party observers, and consequent on the infavourabale results of the recent bye-elections, Congress (I) Supremo, Sri Rajiv Gandhi announced constitutions of, among others, a Cabinet Committee, headed by himself, to monitor the implementation and progress of the Prime Ministers' 20-Pt Programmes, meant for the development of the minorities and other weaker sections of the society. This has been necessitated to prevent the minority communities from being gradually disillusioned towards Congress (I) governments which have, according to the observers, alamost failed to adequately protect their interests causing party debacles.

ABA Ghani Khan Chaudhury, Congress (I) Observer on Tura Lok Sabha seat bye-poll, indicated in his findings, among other things, certain organizational shortcomings, lack of coordination amongst various party leaders and different party units. He has also gone to substantially add his personal appreciation for Sri Purno A. Sangma, Chief Minister of Meghalaya, obviously for his best efforts put in to restore Congress (I) image and in winning the bye-poll with record poll in favour of the party candidate from Tura.

Such and such other party matters apart, it is really heartening to note that Khan Chaudhury also very rightly appreciated the overall sentiment of the rural electorate after his coming into close touch with the leaders of some local organizations, specially the minorities who had, inter-alia, suffered immensely during the last years' violences in the district of Garo Hills.

It may be recalled that starting from the creation of Meghalaya as a separate state in 1972, and barring only half-a-term of the Assembly during 1978-82, the Indian National Congress (INC) has been in an almost uninterrupted grip of powers in Meghalaya and during the entire period of Congress rule, Capt. W.A. Sangma had been heading the Government as an undisputed leader until the last ever memorable term when a youthful and dynamic leader, Sri P.A. Sangma replaced him after the Governor, Sri Bhishma Narayan Singh installed a minority Congress (I) government despite claims staked by the opposition Regional Democratic Front (RDF) following February, 1988 elections.

Meanwhile, in all these years of his (Capt. Sangma's) Chief Ministership, the State marched, undoubtedly, towards progress and prosperity, but for the almost year-long violences during 1987 when all his credibility of equally safeguarding the interests of all communities came into an instantaneous end.

Moreover, as the minority people tend to ascribe to, anti-nontribal policies of his Government such as putting restrictions on transfer of lands, as also on trades and commerce, reservation of government jobs and Assembly seats beyond proportion, denial of all facilities for basic and higher education, financial aids and assistances including bank loans and in such other economic spheres covered under 20-Pt as well as 15-Pt Programmes, which might provide some means to the minority nontribals to earn their livelihood and give bread to a lot of hungry mouths and so forth, have had an extremely adverse impact on these people of the State.

Incidentally, the Constitution of India provides for restrication on transfer of lands from a tribal to a nontribal in order to protect tribal interests, but speaks of no such restriction on transfer of lands between one nontribal and another at all. The Land Trasnsfer Act of Meghalaya, however, puts such an unconstitutional restriction also which, in turn, is apprehended to render the nontribal generation totally landless in not too distant a future since under the Act even transfer of lands inherited is also restricted and is likely to compel them, in course of time, to quit the State or to live without any claim even over a homestead either.

Be that as it may, it is quite irksome, illogical and undemocratic a government action that in Meghalaya 90% of the jobs stand at present reserved for the three main tribes, viz, Khasi, Jaintia and Garos. Accordingly, only 10% jobs are open for the remaining people of the state, and that too handicapped by the requirement of Permanent Resident Certificate (PRC) --- a supersensitive certificate issued after stringent and wearisome process but practically not to be touched or seen by the applicant himself except remaining pleased with some issue number and date.

This means, out of a minimum ten vacancies in a particular establishment, the nontribal will get only one subject to production of PRC, which can hardly be produced due to the facts mentioned earlier, and that the requirement being below ten they (nontribals) entitle to no post at all --- their representation in MCS/MPS and such other services being absolutely zero. It is again quite ridiculous that the only post thus obtainable by the nontribals is to be shared amongst as many as ten different communities, which virtually places them all nowhere in government jobs. Thus, it deprives even the Scheduled Castes and other plains tribes recognized as Scheduled Tribes shortly before also of their legitimate claims over employment in the state.

Such a discriminatory policy of job reservation is deemed not only to be ultra-vires the Constitution but also is absolutely violative of the latest Supreme Court ruling, which categorically states and enjoins upon every state government that not more than 50% of the government jobs shall be reserved.

It may not be out of place to also mention here that the Constitution of India, undoubtedly, provides for every reasonable opportunities including certain special privileges to be given to the backward people for their rapid development, and more so to bring them up into the national mainstream as quickly as possible. However, this may not mean at all that in doing so, (i.e., in bringing up the backwards) the minorities of the State should be plagued with reservation of as nearly as 90% of the jobs and that the minorities should thus be brought down to the level of the backwards to equalize their status.

Can our government bring up the backwards and bring about country's developoment in such a degenerating way, and thus achieve the goal had in mind of the framing fathers of our Constitution ?

Unfortunately, however, such illusive attempts seem to be not beyond plan and policy of our government. But our government should be very much alive to the point that in nurturing one limb, the other limb be not exposed to

any deficiency syndrome likely to occur owing to mal-nutrition, which may contrary to general expectations paralyse the whole process of development and lead to total imbalance and destruction. One can only wish that nothing of the sort happened in Meghalaya as a result of such an imbalance being sought to be created in terms of development and other connected activities.

Needless to say, the sudden outbreak of sporadic violences in Shillong in the month of June, 1987, as also at Tura in August, 1987 rendering thousands of nontribals (Hindus, Muslims and Nepalees) homeless with an almost unspecified loss of innocent lives, not tospeak of burning and pulling down of houses and other losses occurred following its widespread repurcussion all over the state, went out of control due mainly to administrative inaction and total indifference of the Congress (I) leaderships in the state --- a fact which was, at one stage, admitted by the then Union Minister, Sri P.A. Sangma himself after he air-dashed to Tura to survey and take stock of the post-violence situation.

The points as mentioned and the consequent generation of a sense of insecurity in the minds of the nontribals as a whole in the absence of any government help had practically escaped the notice of the three-member Central Study Team sent by our Prime Minister to report on the fallout of the violences despite the clear letter of threat to resign issued by all the five nontribal Congress (I) MLAs of the then Assembly in the event of Capt. Sangma's failure to adequately protect and safeguard the minority interests.

And yet strangely enough, contrary to public expectation, the findings of the aforesaid study team, unfortunately, went against the minority victims of Garo Hills, which, as per newspapers reports, ran as "while Nepalees suffered in Khasi Hills, tribals suffered most in Garo Hills", purportedly done based on misinformation given by those leaders who indirectly fuelled the violence, as also to cover up the Congress (I) government inaction and indifferent attitude towards the minorities.

It is obvious that the study team could not appreciate the actual state of affairs owing to non-survey of all the affected areas, and that the representations submitted by various local organizations including the one of those legislators of the adjoining areas of Assam who had, out of panicky, rushed down to Phulbari (Garo Hills) to see and apprise the visiting members of the study team of the gravity and seriousness of the situation then prevailing in the district, as also for taking appropriate remedial measures were probably not taken into consideration.

The Meghalaya Minority People's Conference (MMPC), which seems to be the lone minority organization of the kind formed on the wake of last years' recurring violence, in their 20-Pt Charter of Demands submitted recently to the State Chief Minister, also to the Congress (I) Observer, Sri Ghani Khan Chaudhury, thus, pointed out many a Govt apathy towards the minorities and urged upon the government to sympathetically consider and fulfill their grievances raised therein.

The MMPC demands, amongst other things, relate to amendment of Land Transfer Act, reservation of job on population pattern, re-enforcement of Article 332(3) that existed before 58th Constitution (Amendment) Act was brought into operation, provision of adequate facilities to the nontribal citizens in terms of education, trades, financial assistances including bank loans, revision of procedure for issue of PRC including creation of a separate district comprising of Mouza No. V & B-Mahal, Mouza No.VI, VII, VIII and part of Mouza No.III of Garo Hills and so forth.

It (MMPC) has also complained of no help or assistance at all whatsoever rendered by the government to the nontribal riot-victims of Garo Hills, and many such victims are said to be still living outside the State who left their hearth and home out of apprehension of fresh violence and torture in absence of the government taking any action for their safe return. This had led to the gradual disenchantment of the minorities towards Congress (I) government which was revealed during the Assembly elections held in February, 1988 itself when all the minority-dominated Assembly Constituencies of Garo Hills went quite surmisingly out of Congress (I) grips.

The memorandum submitted by MMPC leaders appears to have impressed beyond doubt upon the Congress (I) Observer whereupon he reportedly made, among other things, a special mention about the minority grievances in his report to the Prime Minister, Sri Rajiv Gandhi which, unlike the reports of the three-member Study Team indicated earlier, has cordially been hailed by all. Hailed is also with gratitude by all the latest move taken by the Prime Minister to constitute a Cabinet Committee referred to earlier which, it is hoped, under the direct supervision of Sri Rajiv Gandhi will, unless proved to be a corcodiles' tears, considerably benefit the minorities of the state, nay, the country.

There is no doubt why credit should not go to Sri P.A. Sangma for the excellent performance and eventful victory of the party in Tura Parliamentary bye-poll. The fact that the party image, as also admitted in the report of Sri Khan Chaudhury, lost during and after the violence but restored, howsoever little could be, by the able leadership of Sri Sangma, can hardly be obliterated. Credit is also due to him inasmuch as normalcy has been restored and the State once again let to progress and prosperity, which are directly responsible for the victory of Capt. Sangma from Tura Lok Sabha seat. The sincere efforts put in by Sri P.A. Sangma within a couple of months after assuming office of the Chief Minister towards a concerted march and development of the state have succeeded significantly in bringing back public confidence, which the MMPC also admitted with due admiration. The beginning seems to be very good and if the trend is maintained all along, no doubt, the Congress (I) will rule the state smoothly for yet some more years to come.

However, Sri Sangma needs to take a retrospective view and review all policies directly affecting the nontribals and ensure that no basic rights guaranteed by our Constitution to them is snatched away simply to meet the narrow party ends, and that in pulling up the backwards in that manner, no imaginary forwards is pushed into the spiders' net to die down and become food of the spiders. In fact, the state government should provide adequate security to all ethnic group of the society with equal opportunity in all spheres for a concerted development and peaceful co-existence.

One can only wish that our youthful Prime Minister, judged from his personal realization of the needs to look into the problems of the minorities, as also the Chief Minister of Meghalaya shall take all remedial measures in regard to minority grievances, which will not only help them live peacefully with honour and equal dignity along with the majority tribal people but also will take themback into confidence on government's sincerity in protecting their lives, properties and other democratic interests in all times to come.

(Filed to newspapers by A. Islam, 1988)

o0o

Hindu-Muslim Amity in Assamese Society

Mohammed Ali Jinnah claimed, about 75% of the Indian Muslims are convert from Hinduism, while Nehru held it to be around 95% on historical grounds. The Mohammedan invaders, having subdued and subjugated most of the Indian Hindu rulers, had ruled India for about 650 years at a stretch with complete authority, and thereby facilitated a rapid spread of Islam as against the age-old Hindu domination beginning with the mythological era.

The most irksome question of horrible kind of casteism, gruesome untouchability and shabbiest form of inequality existing between various groups of Hindu people aside, factors inimical to racial integrity, such as the war prisoners (Hindus) being looked down upon and treated as outcasts by the Hindu society, had led a lot of Hindu ancestors to embrace Islam, which paved the path of Islam gaining a gradual ground in all parts of the country. Besides, the Muslim invaders, who brought not their women with them, taking local wives and thereby increasing their progenies had also added substantially to the percentage of such converts, and consequentially to Muslim population in India.

And with the stepping in of the Mohammedans since Md. Bin Bakhtiyar invaded Assam as back as in 1206 AD, followed by numerous other Mohammedan invaders, a similar process of conversion and spread of Islam came about in this sub-Himalayan land of aboriginal tribesmen as well, and it opened wide the channels of a gradual racial/religious metamorphosis, followed by a fast-growing socio-cultural fusion between the Assamese Hindus and Muslims, and thereby caused them to live, in the years that rolled by, harmoniously with an equal sense of amity, fraternity and peaceful co-existence.

All such expeditions, which witnessed defeat and victory both, left behind a lot of Muslims either by way of their being placed in charge of the conquered land or as captives of the existing rulers. And the Muslims, thus, left behind to live in Assam, like those taking Indian wives as aforesaid, did as well equally take local wives, and including those who might have, in the course of time, become subjects to the Ahom rulers remained in Assam permanently. Sahabuddin Talish, a noted historian, after his visit of Assam during Mirjumla's invasion in 1661, put on record thus :

"It is said that certain inhabitants of this country who bear the name of Mohammedans are descendants from the captured soldiers of that army….. the Mussalmans who had been taken prisoners in former times and had choosen to marry there, their descendants are exactly in the manner of Assamese and have nothing of Islam except the name, their hearts are inclined far more toward mingling with Assamese than towards association with Muslims."

In any case, at one stage, the Muslims had merged and blended themselves with the ruling class so intimately that it became very difficult enough to identify and single them out from the Assamese stream of Hindu gentry. Instances are replete as to many a Muslims having born as well as died as Muslims but did follow nothing of Islam for all practical purposes, and were named with all Hindu denominations, viz, Jogai, Kupeswar, Didai, Podo and so forth. It is said that there was no Mosque worth-the-name, and Muslims had most delightfully taken part in Ujapali in their capacities as Dhulia, Kalia, Uja and so on.

This is further borne out by Dr. S.K. Bhuyan's "Swargodeo Rajeswar Singha" wherein he wrote in clear terms as under:

"The Assamese Muslims had, like the other Assamese subjects, merged and blended with the Assamese nationality. They had no other racial difference with the Assamese except the religious one."

In fact, during the period there emerged a new kind of Muslims. The Muslims, having traditionally mingled and conducted various kinds of inter-action with the Assamese Hindus, had built up a most insignificant Muslim society, symbolical of a crudest form of Islamic culture taking a gradual root with an inbuilt appeal and imposing futuristic impact in Assamese society.

In years that followed, and more so with the advent and Islamic propagation of the Muslim Peers and Fakirs, as also the Bengal stream of people having inflated Assam during the fag end of the British rule and consequent shooting up of the Muslim population, there occurred a genuine revival in the domain of Islamic culture, which opened a new vista of religious fervour and dawned upon the Assamese Muslims as eye-opener toward spiritual uplift and cultural advancement.

And yet the royal patronage received by the Muslim Peers and Fakirs in freely preaching Islam and establishing various Dargahs, Mosques and Majars and revenue-free lands allotted by the Mughal Emperor, Aurangzeb for construction of Hindu Maths and Mandir like that of Umananda near Guwahati, are but all the living testimony of religious tolerance practized by the rulers of both the communities despite a long-drawn Ahom-Mughal rivalry and frequent battles fought between the two.

Even Vaishnava Guru, Sri Sri Sankar Deb himself was also in favour of practicing such religious tolerance and magnanimity as can be observed from Chanda Khan, having been allowed to freely practice Vaishnavism inspite of his being a Muslim religionist, and thereby contributed towards strengthening Hindu-Muslim unity and lasting amity in Assam.

The contribution of the Muslim Peers and Fakirs towards enriching the Assamese literature by composing in Assamese those Jikirs and Jaris and popularizing them amongst the Muslim gentry are simply unparallel. Besides, the Mohammedan Officers who had adored the royal court in their capacities like professional deciphers of Urdu and Persi correspondents did also have no less contribution in this regard.

In this context, the name of Ajan Fakir is remembered with love and reverence by Hindus and Muslims equally, who not only learnt Assamese himself but also composed those Jikirs and Jaris, which are very lovingly sung by Hindu-Muslim both till today. He again forgot not to include in most ornamental fashion various Urdu and Persi words in his creations, and the Vaishnava poets followed suits in this regard with a view to bringing about a literary fusion. The epoch-making spiritual mission so undeertaken had inspired and appealed to Hindus and Muslims equally to come closer to each other and thereby forge unity and an everlasting sense of universal brotherhood. The legend is survived by various magnificent religious structures established by those revered Peers and Fakirs down the generations.

Earlier, Tughril Khan, during his victorious Assam invasion, constructed the first ever Mosque in Guwahati in 1257. It is said that the Mosque at Pua Mecca (Hajo) was constructed by Giyasuddin Awalia, who brought a little earth from the holiest shrine of the Muslims, Mecca, and laid the foundation of this Mosque. It stands at a place where Vaishnava Satras and other Hindu Mandirs also do exist side by side, which signifies but a traditional racial cohesion maintained by our people.

This very holy shrine of Pua Mecca and various other Durgahs like the Durgah of Panch Peers at Dhubri are visited by all with love and equal respect, and can be deemed to have become the prominent shrines of spiritual congregation and confluence of both the communities. The Mosque constructed at Rangamati by the Nawab of Bengal again apparently bears the symbolic significance and impact of Mughal sculptures.

The Muslims had also been conspicuous by their honesty, sincerity, patriotism and sacrifices to the extent important military commands were entrusted by the Ahom rulers upon them as well, besides those having been placed in the royal court in different capacities. Here the name of Md. Ismail Siddique, alias, Bagh Hazarika, whose military genius and heroism is said to be partly responsible for the success of Lachit Borphukan's operation against Ram Singha at Saraighat, deserves special mention.

Incidentally, Bagh Hazarika apart, a lot of other brave Mohammedans are also said to have, along with the Assamese Hindus, unitedly resisted the succeeding Mohammedan invaders, which symbolizes but an all prevailing sense of oneness and single nationality, as also their indefatigable sacrifices and patriotism toward defending their motherland in times of common national crisis.

Back to literature, the Muslim poets of modern Assamese and such other writer like Sufi Saheb, Syed Abdul Malik and so on, have had no negligible a contribution towards building a harmonious social and literary bondage between the Assamese Hindus and the Muslims. It may be worth-noting that in the nineth generation of the great Muslim patariotic hero, namely, Bagh Hazarika mentioned above, was born an equally great and reputed poet, Mofizuddin Ahmed Hazarika, whose poetic and literary genius and contributions including those of a numerous other prominent Muslim literatuers and personalities are but all commendable in the history of Assamese literature.

Accordingly, the present Assamese literature seems to have assumed a unique form of mutual literary adventure, as is borne out by an increased number of Assamese learners and speakers even amongst those Bengali-speaking Muslims, who had hitherto been subject to the Bengali culture and were speaking and learning Bengali language both within and outside the schools and colleges. In fact, Assam can never forget their generous support extended for introduction of Assamese as the official language of the State during late sixties.

Meanwhile, speaking about the contemporary Assamese Hindus, Sahabuddin Talish remarked that despite all prevailing customary prohibitions, the Assamese Hindus did not abstain from eating ghee as a food habit of the Muslims --- while the cultural influence of both the communities upon one another is apparently noticeable to the extent the by-products of ghee and other accessories, i.e. Polao, Kurma etc. are unhesitatingly eaten by the Assamese Hindus, and in like manner, Khar, Kharuni, Ghila-pitha, Chunga-pitha etc. --- the food habits of the Assamese Hindus --- adopted and eaten very ambitiously by the Muslims till this day.

Also, in fine, the impact of Mohammedan art, craft, music, dresses including various behavioral influences on the Assamese Hindus and vice-versa are obviously felt in very walk of their life. Hence, it has been possible on their part to maintain down the ages their racial/religious cohesion both in the past and present except for some sporadic stray incidents of mutual distrust and evil effects that had in recent times raised their ugly heads too sparsely to disturb the age-old communal harmony between the two communities uptil now.

(Filed to newspapers by A. Islam in 1991)

o0o

Birth & Death Registration in Assam

With a view to improving the Civil Registration system, the Government of Assam, from January, 1987, switched over the Registration hierarchy from the GPs to the PHCs/CHCs etc. In the rural areas , and from the Municipal Medical Officers (MOs) etc. to the Urban Health Officers (UHOs) in the urban areas respectively. Accordingly, the MOs in the rural areas and UHOs in the urban areas within some specified jurisdiction are designated as Registrars of Births and Deaths, upon whom may lie the overall responsibility for effective implementation of civil registration in the state.

Meanwhile, the government also introduced the notifiers system in keeping with the provisions of the Registration of Births and Deaths Act, 1969 for notifying every birth and death event to the Registrars. In this regard, the VHGs, ANMs, SIs, Keepers and Chowkidars of cremation or burial grounds were specified as the notifiers. Moreover, the MPWs in the sub-centres have also been designated as sub-registrars in their respective areas for keeping a close link between the registrars and the notifiers.

Presumably, the spirit and inevitability behind designating the MPWs as sub-registrars for keeping a link between the Registrars and notifiers was foreordained to also ensure that the notifiers - 90 per cent of the rural population having been flatly apathic in reporting and registering all birth and death events on their own owing to illiteracy and ignorance – did not at all default themselves in executing their duties entrusted by the government.

Such being the case, and the actual intention behind switching over the registration hierarchy to the Health department having been to facilitate effective administrative control over the performance of the registration machinery, it was certainly expected that the responsibility of unfailing reporting of all birth and death events would be enjoined upon the notifiers themselves by way of stern disciplinary action and by imposing penalty on the defaulting notifiers through strict administrative superintendence.

Unfortunately, however, and contrary to the general expectations, it is learnt that an element of compulsion making production of birth certificates obligatory on the part of the people for admission in academic institutions, inclusion of names of the children in ration cards, obtaining loans, subsidies and other government grants including enrolling one's name in the electoral rolls, which incidentally, has become so important a document now-a-days for establishing one's nationality or citizenship, is on the anvil and being introduced also shortly in the State.

Such a move is viewed with serious concern inasmuch as it will adversely affect the illiterates and other under-privileged people of the society. Further, most of the rural populace is still ignorant about such a legal necessity. Thus, they being simply averse in this regard, such a compulsion, unsuitable to our society, will intensely arm the notifiers and other connected staff with an edgy weapon to undercut the underlying principles, and defeat the very purpose of civil registration by way of undue harassment and exploitation of the poor and guideless rural masses.

It is obvious that there is every possible apprehension of unnecessary harassment and economic losses of the rural masses leading to increased corruption and loss of people's faith on the system, the people being required to attend the registration centers for days together for a single registration and issue of birth or death certificate, in the event of imposition of such compulsion on the people.

However, since the principal object of Civil Registration System is an unhindered collection of population statistics without public inconvenience, the government may, therefore, considered incorporation of the following points in the Assam Registration of Births & Death Rules for effective implementation and their promotion in the state.

a)

It may be made obligatory on the part of all the notifiers to undertake a house-to-house visit for collecting birth and death events and to obtain the duly filled in and signed registration proforma prescribed in this regard. This will bridge the gap between the reporting and registration process and reduce all delays and public hardships;

b)

The notifiers may be entrusted with the undefiable duty of preparing and submitting a weekly report to the registrars (if necessary, a nil report to the effect) covering their respective areas within the stipulated time without fail;

c)

The Sub-Registrars should maintain a strict supervision over the functioning and performance of the notifiers, and to ensure that the notifiers do not default in executing their duties,and he may conduct a monthly village visit. He must report back his findings to the Registrars;

d)

Based on the findings of the Sub-Registrars so reported, action may be initiated by the Registrars against the defaulting notifiers, if any who should be penalized wherever necessary. This will drive the defaulting notifiers back to their sense to duty;

e)

All the reported events may be duly entered in the B&D Registers maintainable in all such registration centers within a week's time from the date of their receipt. A strict supervision and vigilance many also be maintained on the dealing staff to ensure that no corruption can take place. It should also be seen that no one need attend the registration centre for a number of days for recording a single birth or death;

f)

A special cell for receiving complaints and other public

grievances against the notifiers or other staff concerned with registration work may be opened in each of the registration centers. The complaints so received may be enquired into and action take expeditiously by the Registrar;

g)

In the urban areas too improvement of the existing systems may be effected suitably on similar lines so as to put an end to the corrupt practices, undue public harassment and exploitation which may take place in any form indicated earlier;

h)

Towards this noble end, government needs to suitably enhance the manpower in various stages of the registration hierarchy with necessary provision for funds duly devised in the State Budget or with financial assistances from the Centre. This is required for giving suitable additional incentives to the health worker to compensate them and make them feel happy doing their jobs sincerely and more effectively;

i)

In any case, a separate branch with independent staff and workers for the civil registration, if created, will go a long way in promoting effective implementation of the civil registration system, without any hindrance to the independent work of different health workers at different level also.

(Published by A. Islam & others, The Sentinel, dated March 6, 1988)

o0o

Health-Care & AMSA Agitation in Assam

Be it the trade union or a service association, going on in for a recurringly massive strike has, in fact, become almost an order of the day. It has again posed a really dreadful threat, like some incurable and malignant malady, to the very credibility of the government either in containing them or in maintaining any discipline and order amongst different cadres of employees for the larger interest of the people in particular and the State as a whole.

The kind of malady has caught not only the general stream of employees but also has, of late, infected the doctors, especially in Assam with almost "an unassailable impunity". I call it "an unassailable impunity" because of the godlike image, and capability of the doctors, who may, as in mythology, keep a man alive as long as wished and, if not able to do so, can prevent the "Jamraj" and defer death to some later date at the least, and that as such they tend to be completely unmoved by all other forces --- human and spiritual equally.

As a matter of fact, the actual intention of saying so is not to hurt the doctors' sentiment but only to admit unequivocally that doctors do stand as the saviours of life next only to God, and are thus looked upon in a like manner most. Despite this towering image, what might be absolutely unbecoming of such a professional is that far from being humanistic, frequent strikes etc. resorted to by the doctors in association --- involving at times enormous human sufferings and avoidable cost of precious lives --- does show an all time stubborn attitude of theirs with potential threat to a fair health-care to our suffering masses.

All this again points at but utter helplessness of the administration in taking a hardened stand for curbing such unconducive practices in like manner as was done recently in curbing the strikes resorted to by All Assam Karmachari Parishad. It so happens because the strikes by general employees do not affect public life as intensely as that of the doctors. It is for this unsurfaced but nevertheless reasonable apprehension that it may be scarcely possible to run even a single hour without doctors' services, Government is seen often to remain dumb-shelved at the merciless strikes resorted to by the doctors.

But then the doctors too have their own problems and reservations. It is obvious enough that they too are the unescaped victims of various government neglects and indifferences in terms of their service conditions and other vagaries like working day in and day out and attending patients on Sundays and other holidays, that too without any extra remuneration. Naturally, lack of a fair deal and adequate incentives leads to their moral degradation and resultant poor quality of their services including resorting to frequent strikes etc.

One wonders that non-availability of doctors in hospitals and dispensaries during duty hours or so is a marked feature while public chit-chats and complaints on such affairs are not quite unoften heard of, which enable us a good deal to guess and gaudge the quality of their services being rendered to the suffering milieu. It so happens because a good number of doctors are seen mostly to remain busy after obtaining transfers and postings occasioned mostly under ministerial interference or so. As a result, health problems might perpetuate and remain as problems for good. One can unstrivingly notice that despite a rapid increase in the number 108

of doctors every year, their shortage is felt all the more, particularly in rural areas, that too at a time when the world is heading for surplus doctors ranging from 1500,000 to 500,000 lakhs by 2000AD.

Equally responsible for the poor quality of doctors' services and the sorry state of health-care in Assam may be the occasional non-supply or shortage of some of the essential items of medicines and lack of other modern facilities in different hospitals and dispensaries. If the versions of different patients and even of some doctors in-charge of certain medical or health institutions are to be relied on, non-supply or irregular supply of medicines constitutes a major stumbling-block on the path of fair health-care in Assam, and leaves an adverse impression in public mind on doctors' integrity and honesty including quality of their services rendered.

In this context, it may be worth-while to mention that Tuberculosis, being one of the most fatal diseases, some special national programme, namely, National T.B. Control Programme, among others, has been launched and is presently in full operation throughout the country. The nation as a whole is learnt to incur an annual expenditure on this score to the tune of Rs. 2000.00 lakhs approximately. The Government of India and the concerned State Government provide funds for supply of free medicines to such suffering patients on a 50:50 basis. Unfortunately, in Assam not all the components, viz, IHH (Isonex), Thioacetazone, Ethambutol tablets and Streptomycin injections, are always available at a time in all the hospitals or dispensaries, not to speak of other kinds of medicines. Such irregularities render the patients permanently incurable because of certain "desultory effects" or medically speaking "resistance" said to be created due to taking of one and not taking of another component by the patients.

It seems, therefore, that not only the doctors but also the department are equally responsible for such a sorry state of affairs obtaining in a state like Assam where, besides 64 medical college and other hospitals in all, at least 56 CHCs,

436 PHCs, 311 Dispensaries and 5019 Sub-Centres are presently functioning in rural areas, and are being manned by approximately 3000 doctors.

There is no doubt that the numbers of doctors and health institutions are not quite inadequate. But all the rural health infrastructure, chiefly empty hospital buildings or bare laboratories, are gripped by the unhealthy practice of appointing doctors against a particular hospital/dispensary, the house building of which might yet be under process of construction or so, and attaching them with an urban area hospital. This flouts all norms in terms of requirement and strength of the hospital concerned and belies the lofty claim of the government of having established an effective health –care system in the State, except that it is a mere eyewash to deserve any consideration at all, far less to receive any appreciation whatsoever.

As against these backdrops and given the succeeding discussions it will be apparently clear that although doctors are expected to play a very vital role in ensuring effective health-care in Assam their potential could not perhaps be adequately tapped for lack of mutual cooperation and understanding between the Government and the AMSA.

In this context, the current phase (4th in chronological order) of AMSA agitation with a clarion call for a total cease-work for an indefinite period starting from October 3 does arrest public attention since it involves life and death questions of an uncountable suffering human beings throughout the State. If one could look behind, it would be found that this very phase of AMSA agitation is the inevitable outcome of not only decades-long government neglect suffered by the doctors in terms of their various grievances but also of repeated bureaucratic betrayals occasioned time and again during the course of AMSA agitation and needs to be viewed from that perspective as well.

It may be noted that AMSA has been agitating and pleading with the government for amelioration of the service conditions of the doctors and for improvement of hospital facilities including regular supply of medicines and increase of diet money for indoor patients since 1979 itself. Although the then Janata Government headed by Chief Minister, Golap Borbora did show some positive gesture by allowing doctors to undergo P.G. studies on deputation etc., the successive government is, however, said to have hoodwinked them and much to the doctors' frustration backed out from those assurances and benefits extended by the previous Janata Government.

Meanwhile, AMSA's unrelented fight with occasional strikes, demonstrations, and resentments was intensified during the AGP regime. In fact, AMSA had adopted both persuasive and coercive (democratic) methods to win over the government in realizing their grievances.This had culminated in a broad agreement on November 9, 1989 reached between AMSA on one hand and Sri A.P. Sarwan, Chief Secretary of Assam and some other concerned bureaucratic heads on the other. This very agreement was deemed to be a major achievement on

AMSA's part as it spelt out a definite set of assurances with specific time-frame within which the AMSA demands, viz (a) Deputation of doctors for P.G. studies, (b) Amendment of Service Rules and preparation of Gradation List including publication thereof, (c) Confirmation of doctors after 5 years of services, (d) Supply of medicines and increase of diet money, were to be implemented, but for the Government backing out from its stand and assurances subsequently, the present tangles and problems ensued.

This had perhaps left AMSA with no other option but to issue a time-bound ultimatum for fulfillment of their 5-point Charter of Demands which includes, besides those of the preceding paragraphs, Time-Scale promotion of doctors, Advanced Increments, Incentives for working on holidays etc. In this context, a memorandum was also submitted by AMSA to the then Chief Minister, Sri P.K. Mahanta on September 8, 1990 whose failure to respond positively made AMSA to resort to a four-phased agitation and have successfully carried out its first three-phases, nearing virtually to total cease-work since only "Emergency Services were open during the agitation periods. The last (i.e., the 4th) phase of their agitation was temporarily suspended under the changed political situation in the State.

In the meantime, there was further persuasion with the present Congress (I) government led by Sri Hiteswar Saikia to which AMSA is said to have received a lukewarm response raising their discontentment to a still higher magnitude. Consequently, AMSA has resorted to the

4th Phase of the agitation, temporarily suspended earlier, and their total and indefinite cease-work has virtually paralyzed the whole health-care machinery all through the state. This has led to immense setbacks to the suffering people not only in rural and interior areas but also in towns and cities all over Assam.

It is no denying the fact that there seems to be no human consideration behind such a tough decision on the part of AMSA. is believed, doctors have no friends and foes, nor do they distinguish between the two while treating the suffering persons. Humanity and human services have since long been their prime and foremost consideration against all other consideration--- material or otherwise. The way the AMSA wishes to realize its grievances may not have been backed by any of such human considerations. In any case, the striking doctors too cannot have any peace of mind by not attending a dying patient, nor can derive any satisfaction, should the suffering patients die before their eyes, out of any such effort for fulfillment and realization of their grievances either. Further, this will rather stain their god-like image with an indelible black spot and smear their ethical pyramid altogether.

But then the Government also does not seem to be playing any fair game with the aggrieved members of AMSA. Some of the AMSA demands like supply of medicines and increase of diet money to the indoor patients are really in public interests while the others like the time-scale promotion in the absence of any cadre-wise promotion avenues, advance increments, confirmation, publication of Service

Rules (amendment) and Gradation list etc. also appear to e genuine enough deserving immediate fulfillment. In fact, non-fulfillment of these demands affect their morale adversely and are deemed to be one of the major setbacks towards improving the quality of doctors' services and ensuring effective health-care in Assam.

It may, therefore, be in the fitness of things and the better interest of the suffering milieu that government budged from its stand and considered fulfillment of at least the more genuine grievances of AMSA, if not all, at the earliest possible opportunity. In any case, the government should sit in discussion with the agitating doctors forthwith, sort out things and convince them (AMSA) to call off their indefinite cease-work with requisite immediacy should the suffering patients not die prematurely and the condition of our ailing health-care system not deteriorate further to an irretrievable extent.

(Filed to The North East Times on October 3, 1991 by A. Islam)

o0o

Chapter-VI

Garo Hills-Goalpara-Dhubri

Garo Hills vis-à-vis Goalpara Zamindars

The dawn of the British rule in India saw the once powerful Mughal Empire gradual fall and sink in the dusk during the eighteenth century, and with the ultimate devolution of powers to the East India Company in 1765, the country lying in the western part of Assam down Kamrup district, formerly included in Kamatapur or Koch Kingdom which was already under Mughal occupation then, also came under the British empirical rule.

The district of Goalpara including Garo Hills, comprehended to the four thana areas of Goalpara, Dhubri, Karaibari and Singimari and bounded by the frontier lands of Bhutan (Eastern Duars) on the north, Mymenshingh district on the south, Assam proper on the east and Rangpur district on the west, did also form part of British empire and was originally ruled as part of the permanently settled Rangpur district of Bengal.

This district covered total area of 4,104 sq.miles, of which Singimari than alone appears to have commanded jurisdiction over 1,731 sq. miles, the remaining 2373 sq. miles, i.e. 151,982 acres, have been covered by the other three thanas, and was initially wrested along with Rangpur district by the Mughals from the Koch Raja during the reign of Shah Jahan itself and finally conquered by Aurangzeb in 1660-61.

In Goalpara, the Mughal Government had an officer with the title of Faujdar for collecting revenues and was stationed at Rangamati. Some local magnates, known as Choudhuries, had already established themselves on either side of Brahmaputra and also in the slopes of Garo Hills and enjoyed the estates held by them hereditarily. ? They had to pay mal or revenue, not in cash but in kind to the Mughal Government and enjoyed the estates hereditarily.

Incidentally, in 1893, after the introduction of Zamindari System by Lord Cornowallis, the estates held by these Choudhuris came under permanent settlement while some parts of the district still continued to be settled on periodic leases.

The entire district of Goalpara comprising of a number of parganas of permanently settled estates, thus continued to be managed by these Choudhuris, and according to D.D. Mali, author of Revenue Administration of Assam, there were altogether 19 such estates, later constituted into 9 estates, were permanently settled and wondered himself about the remaining 10 estates as to how they came to be permanently settled.

According to James Bedford, the then Deputy Collector,Goalpara, 12 parganas or estates, viz, Karaibari, Kalumalupara, Mechpara, Habraghat and Khuntaghat of Bijni estates, Goalpara, Dhubri, Chapar, Tarreya,

Goleyalumgunge, Nobad Futoree, Parbat Joyar and Ghurlah (including Mokrampur, Mameerah and Aurangabad), were prominent, among others.

Besides these and some Lakhiraj estates, mention is also found in other source books of some other estates like Sidli, Guma, Ripu, Chirang annexed from Bhutan and also of Rupshi, Bagribari etc. which had either formed part of the above estates or were under separate Zamindars.

Of these, the first mentioned four frontier estates along with Goneseer, Susang and Sheerpur estates in Mymenshingh encircling Garo Hills are claimed to have been, since long back, part of the district (Garo Hills) to which effect there appears to be an undefined dearth of reliable materials, since right from the Koches or even before that these areas have either been included in the Koch Kingdom or that of Padshah of Gaur.

As noted by Gait, Raghu Deb, son of Chillarai, who was in turn brother of the then powerful Koch King, Naranarayan during 15th and 16th century, ruled at Koch Hajo, the other divided portion of Koch Kingdom, Koch Behar. His country included, among others, the country lying between the old course of Brahmaputra and Garo Hills, which now forms part of Mymensingh district. Chillarai, who once waged war against the Padshah of Gaur, was defeated and taken prisoner to Gaur. He, however, gained freedom by flattering and drawing favour of Padshah's wife and married Padshah's daughter. It is said that he (Chillarai) received as dowry of his wife the parganas of Bahirband,

Bhitarband,Gayabari, Sheerpur and Daskunia, i.e., some portion of Rangpur and North Mymensingh.

The present Koch, Rabha and Hajong population dominating the western part of Garo Hills indicate that, contrary to the claim, besides the estates in question a major part of the district was under the Koch Kingdom which bears eloquent testimony to the effect that, these areas might never have formed part of the lands held by the Garos. However, the claim, as mentioned, remains by and large controversial.

Garo Hills, which had no specific administration except some independent Garo chiefs, spread over an area of about 85 miles in length, east to west, and 50 miles in breadth, north to south, i.e., 4,250 sq.miles including the portion covered by the four Goalpara Zamindar estates of Karaibari, Kalumarlupara, Mechpara and Habaraghat (Bijni), had all along been considered as a part of Goalpara district.

The district of Goalpara was separated from Rangpur by Regulation No.X of 1822 covering the aforesaid four thana areas along with Garo Hills, formed into a single district, viz, North East Rangpur, i.e., Goalpara and Garo Hills together and was placed under a Special Civil Commissioner.

According to A.H. Maffat Mills' Report on the Province of Assam, this special arrangement was made with a view to reclaiming the uncontrollable Garo mountaineers who were in the habit of fighting one another and making annual plundering incursions on the plainsmen with extreme cruelty and savagery, and was administered direct in the spirit of Bengal Regulation.

David Scott, who was already simultaneously the Special Civil Commissioner of North-East Rangpur,i.e., Goalpara and Garo Hills, and Judge of Circuit and Appeal in the Zilla of Sylhet, exercising both civil and criminal jurisdiction, was entrusted with the administration of Central Assam also after the Treaty of Yandaboo in 1826 and from this time, according to Sir Edward Gait, the district of Goalpara including Garo Hills, though administered in the spirit of Bengal Regulations, was virtually treated as part of the ordinary jurisdiction of Assam.

During the years 1837-60, both Garo Hills and Goalpara was also administered as a single unit under the Assam Code of 1837. David Scott, who was in-charge of this district, exercised superintendence over the Garo trade also.

In 1866, the Eastern Duars, comprising of the five tracts, namely, Bijni, Sidli, Guma, Ripu and Chirang, lying on the north of Goalpara district and on the foot of Bhutan, were annexed to Goalpara and along with Garo Hills added to Koch Behar Commissionership in 1867.

It may be worth-noting that Garo Hills was, as indicated earlier, placed under a single district of North-East Rangpur with a view to amending the Garo mountaineers and the British Government undertook a strenuous effort to promote peace, harmony and civilization among the Garos by way of non-interference and other measures but frustratingly failed to achieve any tangible result.

In 1869, Garo Hills was formed into a separate district and some peace, howsoever little, could be ensured only after a good number of Garo Chiefs were overpowered and subjugated in an army action in 1871-72.

The whole tract covering Garo Hills and Goalpara including the Eastern Duars was transferred to the newly created Chief Commissionership of Assam in 1874.

Apart from a few Govt Khas Garo Mahals covering an area of about 564 sq. miles settled by a few scattered Garo clans, there was a lone permanently settled estate, namely, Pirpal Baklai estate in the plain portion of Garo Hills near Mohendraganj, while the four frontier estates of Karaibari, Kalumalupara, Mechpara and Habraghat (Bijni) commanding jurisdiction over a pretty stretches of Garo Hills in the interior formed an indispensable part of Goalpara district and were held by Raja Romnath & Radhakisto Lahory (jointly), Pratap Chandra Baruah of Gauripur, Pritheeram Choudhury and Balit Narayan (Bijni) respectively.

These frontier estates were dominated by Bengalis and other non-tribal settlers and collected revenues from the Garos. Some Garo Chiefs paid tributes while some other still remained independent in their internal administration, and that most of the interior places were taken by the British officers to be rather totally uninhabited.

Karaibari, part of which now falls in Bangladesh,

was a large estate (800 sq.miles) covering a major portion of Garo Hills in the south-east, and surrounded by hills and wild jungles into the narrow passages of which no regular troops of the British could penetrate, and along with Mechpara estate (550 sq.miles) stretched, north to south over a tract about 67 miles in length and 23 miles in breadth, while Kalumalupara, sandwiched between the two, covered 133 sq.miles.

These three estates along with Ghurlah (including Aurangabad, Mukrampur and Jamira pargana), which again covered an area of 441 sq. miles, formed Military Tenures and were considered to be the istimary mahals paying revenue on low-rate to the Mughal government on condition of their opposing the Garo mountaineers from raiding the plainsmen.

Habraghat (Bijni) spread over an area of 334 sq.miles and together with the above four covered a total of 2,662 sq. miles and they all together might have commanded jurisdiction in the entire south bank of Goalpara district and pretty over the plains Mouzas, i.e., Mouza No.V,VI, VII & VIII and considerable portion of the hills Mouzas of Garo Hills.

The district of Garo Hills, divided into two portions, i.e., hills portion and plains portion comprised of a number of Mahals, i.e. Nazarana Mahals in the hills portion and Zamindary Mahals in the plains portion and included both Khas and Zamindari lands.

While both annual and period leases including house tax in jhum tenures were in vogue in the hills portion, lands held in the plains portion, however, were either permanently settled or settled on annual leases in respect of Khas as well as Zamindari lands.

Periodic leases were introduced in the plains portion only in 1906-08 covering Mouza No.VI, Mouza No.VII and Mouza No.VIII. The Zamindari lands, having mostly been included in the above-mentioned four frontier Goalpara Zamindari estates, 75% of revenues collected in Garo Hills were received by these Zamindars and the rest gone to the Government exchequer.

According to Mills, out of the four thanas including two Police Out Posts at Salmara and Kurmarpeta, thana Singimari, besides a usual police detachment, was the headquarters of a Garo Surbarkar, i.e., Superintendent of Garos, who along with the Garo polices stationed at various hats, viz, Tikrikilla, Bangalkata, Rajabala, Singimari, Kakripara, Puthimari etc. collected revenues from the Garo Nokmas and was responsible for ensuring law and order including peace and tranquility amongst the Garos.

It is also learnt that at the time of creation of a separate district in 1869,Singimari was made into the district headquarters of Garo Hills initially but shifted to Tura at a later stage, and the thana office had also been shifted to Phulbari from Singimari for administrative conveniences.

Since Independence, the rights of Zamindars have been abolished. During the sixties, when the APHLC movement for a separate hill State was in its peak and gaining greater momentum, a feeble voice was raised by a section of Non-Garo people, either for inclusion of those four frontier estates in their entirety to the State to be carved out of Assam or to retain them with the original jurisdiction covering part of Garo Hills with Assam itself apparently for fear of being placed in total isolation from most of their kith and kins living in Assam and, may be, more so owing to the inherent apprehension and past experiences of the Garo cruelty and outrageousness meted out on their ancestors from time to time, but failed to evoke any tangible result.

To conclude, let me venture to add that Meghalaya was created in 1972 with two hill districts, namely, Garo Hills and Khasi & Jaintia Hills rendering the non-Garo settlers of part of those four Zamindari estates, now in Garo Hills, ever outside the domain of Assam whose ethnic relation is more akin to Assam than to that of the hill sate of Meghalaya. Over the last few decades, there has been a considerable improvement in the Garo-Nongaro relationship, and a pure assimilation and an unfettered sense of brotherhood and mutual understanding would have grown further on a firm and lasting basis but for the recent disturbances and mounting communal tensions all over Garo Hills, it will take probably yet another long spate of time to recoup and restore confidence and mutual trust amongst various section of the people living in the district for lasting peace and harmonious co-existence.

(Published By A. Islam, The Shillong Times, dated January 24, 1988)

o0o

Garo Hills In Retrospect

(Pre-Independence Era)

The British government had constituted the district of North-East Rangpur,i.e., Goalpara and part of Garo Hills together, under Regulation X of 1822, and placed it under David Scott, the first Special Commissioner of North Eastern Frontier of Bengal. This arrangement did not, however, affect the lands actually held by the independent Garo Chiefs, known as Garowana, in the interior hills.

Keeping in view the overall British policy of territorial expansion, David Scott subjugated as many as 121 independent Garo Chiefs in these hills bordering North-East Rangpur and Mymensingh, and thus laid the foundation of British Administration in this hilly homeland of the Garos.

The British government did not deem the Garo race to be of any competence, and considering them less reliable and more so, in view of the risks of direct intervention in their social life, the district was initially administered as an excluded area, mostly from outside, i.e. from Goalpara. This had caused manifold difficulties in carrying out the administration with effective control over the Garos, and thus, a separate administrative unit, viz, Garo Hills, had to be created.

Garo Hills was, thus, by the Act XXII of 1869, constituted into a separate district, and was placed under Lt. W.J. Williamson. Lt. Williamson, the first Deputy Commissioner of Garo Hills, continued to administer the district as a partially excluded area, and had brought the district under complete British subjugation after the three-sided expedition, conducted in the cold season of 1871-72.

The expedition claimed several lives of patriotic

heroes including late Togan N. Sangma, who very heroically fell before the British bullets in defence of and before parting with the motherland.

Meanwhile, an acute border dispute cropped up leading to serious commotion, claims, counter-claims and protracted movements on the part of the Garos and the neighbouring estate holders or Zamindars. In this context, the name of Sonaram R. Sangma, as the ring-leader of the first ever Garo riyats movement, deserves special mention.

Messers Kelso and Bedford, having conducted a revenue survey between 1849-54, demarcated the southern boundary of North-East Rongpur, i.e., Goalpara district. The Kelso-Bedford line ran close to northern hills of Garo Hills, ignoring which, Mr. Backett, deputed for demarcating the boundaries of the new district, drew a line known as Backett Line, later notified in 1875, far beyond that of the Kelso-Bedford, covering blocks of lands hitherto included in Goalpara district.

Disgruntled at this, the neighbouring estate-holders, from Habraghat to Karaibari, filed civil suits against the government. The squabbling, followed by a protracted negotiations, terminated in the government recognizing the estateholders' claims in 1878. However, the lands, in question, remained ever apportioned to be managed by the Deputy Commissioner, Garo Hills subject to payment of a given percentage of revenue receipts to the respective Zamindars (better known as 10 Annie : 6 Annie lands).

Thus the status of Garo Hills-Goalpara boundary continued to remain almost of that of a regent to a ward (king-designate).

Similarly, claims over the northern Mymensingh by the Garos, and over the north-eastern portion of Garo Hills by the 124

Khasi Raja had also, in later years, created some problems.

Lt. Williamson shifted his seat of administration to Singimari in the latter part of 1856. This place, now better known as Hallidayganj, is situated midway between Phulbari and Garobadha in the plain areas of the district. It had, in addition to a thana office, already had the office of the Garo Sarbarkar or Supdt.of Garos. Thus, Singimari stood as the first headquarters of Garo Hills until shifted to Tura.

Prior to shifting the district headquarters from Singimari, Harigaon Hills or Rangira, covered then already by the Gaolpara Zamandary jurisdictions, was contemplated to be a convenient place for district headquarters. These Hills, referred to as Toorapahar by the British, had a garden raised and a beautiful bungalow constructed earlier by David Scott but considering it unsuitable on many front, Lt. Williamson conducted o\an intensive survey, and finally selected and shifted the headquarters, during 1866-68, to the present site of Tura.

It may be recalled that Garo Hills had no specific administrator prior to the British advent, nor was there any system of an organized Government except some independent Garo Chiefs, better known as Raja commanding allegience and receiving tributes from their respective clans, sub-clans and villagers.

As referred to earlier, the British government placed a Garo Sarbarkar at Singimari for collecting taxes from the tribal chiefs. Some Laskars, duly appointed as Government agent from amongst the Nokmas, helped him. Generally, the most influential Nokma was appointed as Laskar, who wielded effective control over all other Nokmas. As the Laskar might pose potential threat against their traditional authority, the Nokmas did comply him as and when required.

The authority of the Laskars was, however, relegated considerably when the Zamindars of Karaibari, Kalumalupara, Mechpara and Habraghat (Bijni), lying on the hilly frontiers, who were invested with an integrated authority of a Rural Police, a Collector and a Magistrate as well, started exercising their powers. This arrangement, however, did not work efficiently and had to be revised by introducing in its place two new offices in a decentralized manner.

Accordingly, in the hills areas the Government appointed Laskar as the authorized Rural Magistrate and Collector of Revenues, and Sardar as in charge of Rural Police. Similarly, in the plain areas, a Gaonbura exercised combined authority of the Rural Arbiter of disputes and the Rural

Police --- Mouzadars being, inter-alia, in charge of revenue collection.

The Deputy Commissioner, being the sole administrator of the district, maintained the overall supervision over law and order (including police), general administration and exercised judicial authority as well. He was, however, assisted by EAC/SDC in his executive and other functions.

The Garo Hills District Fund Committee (GHDFC) with the Deputy Commissioner as the Chairman, was constituted in 1915, which engrafted some features of modern self-government and introduced an organized system of administration in public life, mainly for the four plain mouzas of the district. A growing consciousness amongst the Garos had already been marked to take root earlier on many occasions. This was far more manifest when, in 1925, the Tura Fund Committee, meant for Tura and the hills mouzas only, had to be constituted following pressing public demand. This had virtually marked the opening of a new era in the annals of the Garos.

Both the Fund Committees raised fund from various

local rates and other receipts within their respective jurisdiction. Accordingly, both the Fund Committees carried out works of general nature. From 1937 onward, however, their functions were re-enumerated and enlarged sufficiently to cover all construction works of school and hospital buildings, roads and other communications, hats, wells, tanks health centers and public asylums including promotion of cultivation, combating epidemics etc.

The Fund Committees, starting from 1915, worked till 1952.Though a great deal of efforts was put in by the British for rousing public awareness, the general public apathy towards self-governing process among Garos remained by and large unchanged due to insignificant growth of education and traditional social and environmental isolation and various other factors.

The bare minimum Garo educated elite including the retired War personnel like Capt. Sangma, B.G. Momin, Emonsing M. Sangma etc., despite some interests could not utilize their genius owing to almost a non-representative character of the Fund Committees. Most of the members of these committees were nominated, and then Deputy Commissioner, in the absence of any election of members, played a pivotal role with an overriding power vested with him over the nominated as well as ex-officio members. In fact even Garo Hills itself was represented in the State Legislature by a nominated member until the first ever Assembly elections held in 1946 in the district.

One is, however, convinced that the consistency of the British rule in Garo Hills and its impact on the life of the Garos is apparently noticeable at least to the extent these primitive people (Garos), having finally come out of their narrow confines, started gradually to react and evince interests in self-governing system by virtue of gradual education imparted by Christian Missionaries and such other factors. Judged from the angle of post-Independence political awakening and united efforts put in by the Garos to assert themselves in local as well as extra-local administration, this very aspecat of the British impact becomes more evident, whereby they (Garos) emerged slowly to dominate the political scene of the district and rule their own affairs themselves with self-respects and equal dignity in future course of history.

(Published by A. Islam, The Sentinel, dated June 11, 1988 and The Shillong Times, August 15, 1988)

o0o

Political Uprising of the Garos

(Post-Independence Era)

As I embark upon the present topic, it may be worthwhile to remind the readers that I had shed some light in an earlier article (The Sentinel,Saturday Fare, June 11, 1988) on the growing socio-political consciousness amongst the Garos. In fact, if I may repeat, formation of the Garo Hills District Fund Committee in 1915, meant exclusively for the plains mouzas, had roused among the Garos an increasing sense of socio0political isolation.

Their gradual understanding about the deleterious effects of such a secluded life, thus, started agitating the minds of the slightly educated Garo elite, who had, meanwhile, developed some sense of responsibility towards their society and people. Thus they gradually came out to fight for the cause of their own race which led again to the formation of the Tura Fund Committee in 1925.

Such factors, including the sense of deprivation growing in their minds in terms of opportunities given to the people in the self-governing process, had led the Garos to assert themselves with renewed zeal and courage. Accordingly, some of the Garo leaders were cast overnight into political limelight, and they succeeded to a large extent in bringing the Garo people under a single umbrella to fight unitedly for their common cause and interests. Gradually a political upheaval took root amongst the Garos, and in the course of time Garo Hills emerged as the seat of an overwhelming political movement towards attaining the larger goal of a separate state for the hill tribes of Assam.

These leaders, through their political maneuverings, thus, first sowed the seeds of Garo unity and formed a political party of their own, viz, the Garo National Council (GNC) in 1931. The GNC, though born could only toddle until 1946, when the party was reorganized and a fresh start initiated. Meanwhile, a unit of the Indian National Congress (INC) was also set up in the Garo Hills in 1947 with Phukan Sangma as president. Prior to this, the INC activities had been confined to the plains areas, formed way back in 1935 amongst the Koch, Rabha and Hajong including the Bengali Hindus and the Muslims.

In the context of administrative changes which took place in India after the attainment of Independence, and the growing consciousness amongst the Garos about their racial backwardness, the GNC members grew increasingly restive in their bid to protect and preserve their racial identity and interests,. Accordingly, they led a delegation to the Bordoloi Sub-Committee demanding, inter-alia, complete administrative autonomy for the Garo Hills district.

The Bordoloi Sub-Committee, appointed in the wake of Independence for studying the specific problem of the hills tribes, recommended for constitution of autonomous district councils for all the hill districts of Assam. Thus came about, in place of the Fund Committee, the Garo Hills (autonomous) District Council into being in 1952 after the same had earlier been included in the Sixth Schedule to the Constitution adopted in 1950.

The move for constitution of an autonomous district council for the Garos had --- before it could finally be concretized --- generated apprehension in the minds of the minority non-Garo communities, predominantly living in the plains and outer hills of the district, about their future in the proposed administrative setup, inviting a similar but counter-move. Accordingly, the Koches, Rabhas, Hajongs, Dalus, Banias including the Bengali Hindus and Muslims of the district raised a deamand for formation of regional council, meaning a separate administrative setup of them quite different from that of the Garos.

Alternatively, a demand for the merger of the entire plains belt of Garo Hills district with the Dhubri subdivision of the then Goalpara district, was also made. In fact, such a claim during the period between the partition of Bengal and passing of the Government of India Act, 1935, was, time and again, put before the Assam Government by the Goalpara Zamnindars of Karaibari, Kalumalupara, Mechpara and Habaraghat (Bijni) estates.

Meanwhile, under the able and astute leadership of Captain W.A. Sangma and some other GNC leaders, an agreement with the non-tribal people of the plains areas, including non-Garo tribals, was arrived at to organize a united force to work together for achieving autonomy for Garo Hills district with specific pledges vowed by the GNC leaders for providing equal rights and privileges to all sections of the people for equal development opportunities.

Thus, the burning question of partition of the Garo Hills came to an end with an agreement besides other assurances, that only non-Garo candidates would be put up in the Council constituencies covering the plains mouzas of the district. Accordingly, an electoral alliance between the GNC and INC --- INC being the sole sympathizer of the non-Garos --- was constituted. The first ever Council elections were held in February 1952, in Garo Hills on the basis of adult franchise, and the first Executive Committee was formed with Capt. Sangma as the first ever Garo Chief Executive Member.

During the late fifties, a spate of political unrest was observed in the Garo Hills. GNC leaders in close cooperation with other hill leaders of Assam vigorously pursued a demand for larger autonomy for the hill districts, followed by the demand for creation of Hill State. This had made the Garo Hills District Congress break the electoral alliance entered earlier and part ways with the GNC, because such a preemptive move was considered to be tantamount to the pulling down of the very foundation on which the alliance stood.

However, this could not divert the course of the movement and hill leaders of Assam, under the stewardships of Captain Sangma, raised their unanimous voice for the creation of the Eastern Hills State.

The movement received greater momentum after a united political party, namely, All Party Hills Leaders Conference (APHLC) was formed in 1960. A host of non-tribal members was also found rallying with the APHLC to thwart the move made by the District Congress under the leadership of Phukan Sangma, and this gave a tremendous boost to the morale of the Hills State Movement leadership.

The movement received its biggest thrust after the historic introduction in the Assembly of the Official Language Bill for recognizing Assamese as the official language in Assam, followed by large-scale sporadic violence --- reminiscent to those of the recent past --- which took place in 1987 in the plains areas of Garo Hills along with other places.

The introduction of the Official Language Bill, followed by the sporadic violence, struck hard the sentiments of both the tribals and other non-Assamese people of the Garo Hills. Some misgivings were also allowed to creep into their minds because of slogans like "Assam for Assamese", which contributed to the development of a fear-psychosis amongst the Bengali Hindus and Muslims including the Garos of the districts. This was very tactfully taken advantage of by the tribal leaders in influencing and bringing the non-tribal people under the APHLC banner with oral assurances of adequate protection and safeguards to be provided to them in the proposed new State.

Meanwhile, Captain Sangma, who had already joined State politics and had been occupying a berth in the Chaliha Cabinet of Assam, resigned in protest along with his other associate for the above mentioned events, and started mobilizing non-tribal support, for his Hills State Movement. Accordingly, influenced by the assurances mouthed by the APHOLC leaders, the Bengali Hindus, other non-Garo Hindus and the Muslims of the district made up their minds to extend full support to and stand solidly by the movement.

Participating in mass rally, organized by APHLC at Tura in January 1967, a large number of non-Garo people (Hindus and Muslims both) were found to express solidarity with Garo Hills to the extent of their being an indispensable part of it. Meanwhile, leaders like Stanley Nichols Roy, General Secretary, APHLC, made known their solemn commitments towards protecting the legitimate rights and interests of all the non-tribal residents in the autonomous districts in the

Hills State during the various sessions of the APHLC, particularly the Shillong and Haflong sessions.

As the hill state movement was nearing its goal, the Garo Hills found itself pulled into a political whirlpool of swirling currents and counter-currents. Among others, Emonsing Sangma, then a Minister in the Assam Ministry, in opposing the division of Assam, threatened to launch a counter-movement. A convention of non-Garo people was also held at Phulbari in January 1967 to oppose the movement.

A feeble voice for the merger of the entire plains belt of Garo Hills with Goalpara district was once again heard but without any ostensible impact. Some sporadic attempts on the lives and properties of Hindu tribes, Bengali Hindus and the Muslims plus student unrest also followed to suppress this new tide. Moreover, leaders like Jahanuddin Ahmed, the then nominated MP from the Dhubri Lok Sabha seat, which then included the Garo Hills, was, in opposing the merger demand, found desperately campaigning in favour of APHLC. This he did with an eye on the elections fought then and to corner the Garo votes for him.

Amidst various such crises, however, the fate of the plains areas of the Garo Hills and that of its non-Garo people was ultimately sealed with the proposed Hill State. After the birth of Meghalaya, a first as an autonomous State in 1969, and later as full-fledged one in 1972, Captain W.A. Sangma became the first ever Garo Chief Minister, the second being Mr. P.A. Sangma from the Garo Hills district of the State, which is no mean achievement for the Garos.

Much has been done, over the last two decades, for development of the Garo Hills as also of the State and its people after the emergency of Meghalaya as a new State of the Indian Republic. One is, however, still to be convinced as to how the assurances of the tribal leaders given to the minority non-tribal people are being kept, or how well their legitimate rights and interests safeguarded. The Hill State movement cannot forget these people but for whose generous support it would not have come such a long way. Only a thorough and fair study of the events that have been taking place after the emergency of Meghalaya as a separate State can throw light on this.

(Published in The Sentinel, Saturday Fare, dated October 8, 1988 By A. Islam)

Demand for plain district in Garo Hills

Demand for creating plain district is gaining greater momentum and figured not quite unsurprisingly during the day-long election campaign undertaken by the chief minister of Meghalaya, Mr. B.B. Lyngdoh in plain areas of Garo Hills on May 11 last. The demand was raised on the wake of 1987 violence under the aegis of Meghalaya Minority People's Conference (MMPC).

The chief minister, B.B. Lyngdoh, who addressed a series of public meetings in different places like Mohendragonj, Hallidayganj, Rajabala, Bhaitbari, Phulbari etc. in connection with the ensuring parliamentary elections, however, declared himself that for the present a plain subdivision was being created by his government to meet public aspirations of the area possibly by June this year itself.

Mr. Lyngdoh, who was highly pleased at the warm reception accorded to him all through his campaign here, received a number of public memoranda, and assured the minority people on his own to create an administrative block and set up a vocational institute as well in plain areas, besides protecting the nontribal interests in the State.

The chief minister was accompanied by some of the cabinet colleagues, namely, Mr. B.G. Momin, Mr. Meriam D. Shira, including the rebel Congress (I) leader and ex-MP, Mr. S.K. Marak and the ruling MUPP consensus candidate for Tura Lok Sabha seat, Mr. I.K. Sangma.

Meantime, the MMPC President, Mr. Samsul Huda lamented in saying that although the government directed the DC, West Garo Hills to furnish necessary feasibility report for the proposed plain subdivision long back, there had been an unduly inordinate delay on his part to act on it.

Earlier, the chief secretary, Meghalaya in a note on May 10, 1990 expressed the desirability of creating a district as well as an administrative block in plain areas in view of compactness including cultural and ethnic affinities of the people there. Mr. Samsul Huda, who also added that such a measure, would bring administration closer to people and benefit about 1.5 lakh minorities of the state.

The district of West Garo Hills is divided into four subdivisions, viz, Ampati, Dadenggiri, Baghmara and Tura Sadar subdivisions. The present administrative arrangement, however, provides not even a single development block exclusively for plain areas.

The district headquarters, Tura including the sub divisional headquarters are all located in some distant hill stations, which suffer from absolute communication bottlenecks. In fact, the entire road communications network remains plagued by frequent disruptions and other vagaries especially during rainy season.

All this but adds to public hardships in attending different offices including courts besides the incidence of increasingly higher bus fares and other incidental hazards that are often posed to human life due to accident-prone road communication system in the district.

In any case, the administration is not easily accessible nor can it (administration) adequately meet the aspirations and needs of non-tribal people by establishing closer and regular contacts with them in plain areas.

According to Mr. Huda, the minority people living in plains areas feel themselves as being increasingly alienated and totally deprived even of bare minimum benefits that accrue from different government schemes and programmes owing to chronic information gap, lack of dissemination and proper implementation thereof, which could be removed and remedied only through a separate administrative unit for them.

The MMPC demands, which are as many as 20 in all point-wise, include, inter-alia, creation of a plain district carving out Mouzas No.V, VI, VII, VIII, B-Mahal and part of Mouza No.III of West Garo Hills district, amendment of Meghalaya Land Transfer Act, dereservation of certain assembly seats, absorption of nontribals in government jobs including MCS and MPS cadres adequately, relaxing restriction on trade licences etc.

The proposed district /subdivision will cover an estimated area of 425.9 sq.km with approximately 1.5 lakh population.

Meanwhile, the MMPC in its latest meeting held on May 15 last and subsequent Press release thereon lodged a strong protest as 'unwarranted' against GDC order No. GDC/LR/59/88/29/32 dated January 29 suspending field mutation of lands, and expressed deep anguish on government failure to declare as Gazetted holiday for the major Muslim festival, Id-Ul-Fitre this year.

It demanded immediate vacation of the GDC order or alternatively, to introduce mobile mutation of lands in order to obviate unnecessary public hardships likely to occur as a result of such action, and appealed to the government for declaring as gazetted holidays on all major Muslim festivals,viz, Id-Uz-Zuha, Muhurram etc. at par the Central Government.

The MMPC also urged upon the government, among others, to provide 15 per cent job reservation for

minorities including free school level education, liberal financial help for books, uniforms, nutrition, etc. scholarships, stipends to the minority student of the state.

(A report by A. Islam, The North-East Times, dated June 14, 1991)

o0o

On Creating a Plain District in Garo Hills

The unfortunate stand, "Garo land meant for the Garos, not an inch shall be spared to the non-tribals", taken by All India Garo Union (AIGU) in a recent conference held at Tura in order only to thwart creating the proposed plain district out of West Garo Hills district of Meghalaya, augurs a clandestine patronage received by them from some or other frustrated political quarters of the state.

Here, it may be pertinent to allude to the editorial comment of "The Meghalaya Guardian" of 27th July wherein the very stance taken by AIGU has rightly been termed as "over reaction" and criticized sharply as "…. That it is only the very naïve among us that will believe the stance is anything other than a move designed to fan the flames of communal passion" in the state.

The editorial has also failed not go deep into the cryptic silence maintained over the issue, inter-alia, by the opposition Congress (I) in the state, and could well foresee its evil intention suggesting that it will swamp into action to pull down the present MUPP government taking plea of its failure to contain the situation once it reaches an apparent point of no return and so on. The alleged pleadings of the former Chief Minister of the state, now Union Minister of State for coal etc., Sri P.A. Sangma in recent meet with the State Chief Minister, Sri B.B. Lyngdoh not to concede the MMPC demand for a plain district and his subsequent silence is also indicative of and confirms such a move lurking in Congress (I) camp.

Be that as it may, what ails one most is that the non-tribal people, who had once in late sixties readily accepted ethnic segregation and embraced the tribal brethren out of mutual trust, love, compassion, goodwill including a sense of fraternity amongst one another only to help fulfill their (tribals) longstanding aspirations, seem to have been reciprocated and rewarded by AIGU in an almost unpalatable manner. The AIGU, who have chosen to outright oppose the proposal for a plain district, should not have forgotten the past before taking such a precipitous decision on the matter.

The history of APHLC led Hill State Movement bears adequate testimony as to the magnanimity shown by the indigenous non-tribal sections towards creating the Hill State of Meghalaya by carving out the then Assam's two tribal dominated districts of Khasi & Jaintia Hills and Garo Hills --- initially as an autonomous state in 1969 and then as a full-fledged state in the spirit of the North-Eastern Reorganization Act 1971.

The non-tribal communities living in the two districts had their own reasons of initially apprehending alienation in the proposed set-up. But they had an undaunted faith and trust on the then tribal leaderships as well. This led them to extend an unqualified support to the Hill State Movement and readily preferred to remain administratively attached and bound up with the Garo, Khasi and Jaintia brethren leaving their major ethnic groups in the chopped out remnant state of Assam itself.

The plain portion of Garo Hills, which formed part of the permanently settled Goalpara district of undivided Assam right from the British period, is a non-tribal dominated area of the district. This part, which has an estimated population of 1.5 lakh, comprises of a number of communities, viz, Bengali Hindus, Muslims, Koch, Hajong, Rabha, Bodo including Garos scattered here and there. However, majority of them belongs to Muslim community. The area of this portion is shown to be 425.9 square kilometers.

It may be noted that despite their firm solidarity with the hill leaders' demand, a miniature section of the non-tribal nevertheless raised a feeble voice of protest rather unsuccessfully against inclusion of the plain portion in the proposed hill state during the period apparently out of fear of future complicacies. In fact, they had even gone to the extent of demanding merger of this portion with Assam's Goalpara district also only to be swept away and pacified by the hill leaders' tactful commitments made notably in their Haflong conference and others in the sixties towards ensuring full protection of non-tribal interests in the proposed set up.

Unfortunately, one could witness violation of the commitments on several occasions in the past and it was no less a person than the present Chief Minister, Sri B.B.Lyngdoh himself, a tribal leader belonging to the old flock, who had to remind his other tribal colleagues on the floor of the Assembly itself right back in 1987 about their commitments once again, without, however, any tangible impact on them whatsoever.

The fact that creating a plain district or a subdivision as the Chief Minister, Sri B.B. Lyngdoh reportedly agreed during his last election campaign in the plain areas will not perhaps cause the heaven to fall down, far less to affect any tribal interests. Even those who are up to oppose the proposal at all costs will perhaps agree this. Since the demand is only for a district and nor for a state, the plains will nonetheless remain an integral part of Meghalaya as against AIGU's vague apprehension of losing or parting with it altogether.

Contrary to such apprehensions, it is likely to benefit even those unfortunate Garos, who are living in the foothills adjacent to the plains and could not have over the years accrued any benefit out of the present administrative arrangements, which, incidentally, was devised in a manner to intensify development activities in the interior hills only rather than in the plains or the foothills.

During the two decades-long history of its separate existence, Meghalaya has marched far ahead and developed rapidly in different spheres. So have changed the landscapes and the tribal life basically for whose development this tiny hill state was brought into being about 20 years back. All this could again be possible for a wise and careful management of administration by successive governments and more so because the administration has been brought considerably closer to the tribal people for their faster development.

The two districts of K&J Hills and Garo Hills of the state had soon after its creation been reorganized into five separate districts. Accordingly, Garo Hills district was divided into two separate districts, namely, East & West Garo Hills. So have been the cases with the civil subdivisions and blocks as well. All these measures have also been substantially responsible for increasing pace of development of the state and its people.

The administrative reorganizations made so far have, no doubt, benefited the tribal communities. But, as also noted earlier, it has squarely failed to do equal justice to the non-tribal including the Garos living in the plains and foothills of Garo Hills. In any case, the plain portion, which now falls within Dadenggiri Subdivision of West Garo Hills district, has remained ever neglected on all fronts as against many other places including its immediate neighours of Assam enjoying all modern day development benefits.

The district and sub divisional headquarters, both of which are situated in some far hill stations, are not easily accessible to people of these areas, besides being handicapped by undeveloped communication system and incidence of increasingly higher bus fares and such other vagaries. People of the plain portion cannot attend the district offices including the courts as conveniently as they ought to have. On the contrary, they have to suffer detention or visit offices for days together for a single purpose. Thus, it is evident that they cannot easily reach the administration, nor the administration can maintain a regular and closer contact with these people due to frequent communication disruption and so on and so forth.

Even the smallest administrative block meant for the plain portion is also located in some interior hilly place. As a result, people suffer from various information gap and consequently get deprived even from the barest schematic benefits extended from time to time both by the Central and State Government for public development.

The birth and growth of Meghalaya Minority Peoples' Conference (MMPC) --- the only organization seeking to defend and further the non-tribal interests --- in 1987 and its subsequent demands, amongst others for creating a plain district etc. is the culmination of more than two decades-long neglect and a sense of alienation developed in the minds of the people here. The demand is, undoubtedly, based on genuine needs for equal development and represents public aspirations for getting closer to administration. This seems also to be justified

viewed from the angle of different problems faced by these people and more so for allaying non-tribal apprehension or feeling of alienation developed over the years. In any case, the initial apprehension and current sense of alienation of the non-tribals of the state were/are not without any basis and the AIGU stance opposing the proposal for a plain district is a confirmation and burning example thereof.

There is, in fact, no case whatsoever on the part of ourtribal brethren, especially the Garos, to feel panicky as to losing or parting with their land to non-tribals or so. Even if a plain district is created, which will, in any case, be the sixth district only of the state and not a separate state, no land is to be transferred, and hence such an unnecessary panicky and hue and cry thereon will only create an atmosphere of distrust and fan the flames of communal violence amongst various sections of people in the state. We are aware that the state witnessed communal frenzy on several occasions in the past, causing loss of lives and property equally. Hence it should not repeat in any future for greater interest of the state. There must be some subtle forces trying to exploit our sentiment. But let us not fall prey to their evil design and thwart them unitedly.

"Live and let live" be the motto of our people in order to widen the path of harmonious coexistence. Let us not lose sight of our beautifully glorious past when both tribals and non-tribals of the state cherished to live in an atmosphere of peace, confidence and mutual trust lest we should fall apart and enter a gloomy future.

(Published in The Meghalaya Guardian, dated August 20, 1991 By A. Islam)

o0o

Garo Hills vis-à-vis Dhubri Border Areas

Viewed from the angle of defence and security of the country, the entire international border between India and Bangladesh touching the State of Assam, though not sensitive enough, concerns us considerably, nonetheless.

It has already been engaging our attention time and again over the influx of foreigners and other connected problems. And situation both in Punjab and Kashmir having taken a dramatically intriguing turn, now it has necessitated, besides taking adequate security measures, a very cautious dealing with the people living in the border sector, who have, incidentally, a clear ethnic and linguistic affinity with their immediate Bangladeshi counterparts.

Of the two Bengali Hindu and Muslim dominated districts of Dhubri and Karimganj having a border of about 205 KM in length with Bangladesh, Dhubri district, lying in the western extremity of Assam and comprising of two subdivisions, viz, Dhubri (Sadar) subdivision and Hatsingimari subdivision alone covers about 125 KM.

Incidentally, these two subdivisions each falling on either bank of river Brahmaputra, constitute two separate border sectors, namely, Dhubri and Mankachar sectors. The Mankachar sector, which falls in Hatsingimari subdivision, occupies a border length of about 51 KM.

The Hatrsingimari subdivision, almost sandwiched between Bangladesh on the west and Garo Hills district of Meghalaya on the east --- touched by Brahmaputra and Goalpara district partially on the north-east --- covering about 90 KM in length and with an average breadth of 4 KM, spreads over a small chunk of about 683.5 sq.km in area.

The inter-state boundary between Assam and Meghalaya on the east and the international border on the west having joined together at Sadartilla in the extreme south, the subdivision looks somewhat like a big delta, leaving it with virtually no southern boundary at all.

The population density being 600 people per sq.km, it has an estimated population of around 5 lakhs now.

Needless to say, it is one of the most neglected and backward areas in the State. People here are extremely poor and seem to be living in the Middle Ages.

Ironically enough, in the entire area, covered by two Assembly Constituencies, only one Arts College at Mankachar and a few other schools scattered here and there are imparting education to the upcoming generation.

As a result, it has an abysmally low overall literacy rate of 12.7% with that of woman being 5.7% as per 1971 Census.

The only ITI meant for this area for vocational (technical) education is also functioning from Gauripur --- a place located far away outside the subdivision.

Educationally backward as they are, the people of the area are also especially unconscious to keep up with the fast changing pace of the present dynamic world.

Almost unenlightened on any aspect of government schemes and programmes, a great majority of the educated youth also lack moral courage to extract benefit being extended by the administration, far less to speak about undertaking any private venture on their own.

Further, no political leader worth-the-name is available to enlighten and guide the people in the right direction. Consequently, they are still groping in the dark and could benefit much less even in the sphere of medical services owing to poor health infrastructure facilities, non-availability of doctors at times when the country is set to achieve the goal of "Health For All By 2000 AD".

No industries, small or large in scale, have come up over the years in any part of the subdivision. As a result, the headlight of progress and principal avenues of employment stand totally shut off and out of sight.

The only employment opportunities that had arisen consequent to the creation of this subdivision right back in 1983 is also unavailable now because most of the offices are filled with outsiders; some of them functioning from the district headquarters while yet many others like the judicial court, treasury, Khadi & Gramodyog Board etc. are yet to start functioning.

The Sub-divisional Employment Exchange shows an up-to-date registration of about 6000 educated unemployed, but far greater number of such unemployed persons do not even bother to register their names due to the direct recruitment system being followed by most of the offices.

While the so-called district CRC is alleged to have appointed not even a single candidate from this area on one plea or another, its representation in the Assam Secretariat is absolutely nil and that in the various Directorates and other offices including the ones functioning in the district headquarters is few and far between.

In any case, the number of venture school teachers is disproportionately high here, who hopefully await years to receive grants, aids and such other government assistances in the absence of any other employment avenues.

The communication network is virtually non-existent and provides a maximum motorable PWD road of 26 KM in length to maintain linkage with the district headquarters at Dhubri located on the other side of Brahmaputra. A single ASTC bus operates to connect it with the State Capital, Guwahati --- a distance of about 269 KM. The only other such bus available plies in the Goalpara-Mankachar route that too without a full-fledged station in the subdivision.

The post and telegraphs and telecommunications network including news media like Radio, TV and Press also have given no coverage to the problems of the area so far. Consequently, the SDO (Civil) himself runs without a telephone, not to speak of a telephone exchange in the subdivision.

The Bangladesh Television exercises absolute sway here due to greater proximity and functioning of a high power TV transmitter there as against the low-power Indian ones from which reception is extremely bad.

The entire area is inter-spersed with various chars and is criss-crossed by different tributaries of Brahmaputra. Hence, there is hardly any scope for group farming, although agriculture is the mainstay of the sub divisional economy. In fact the area is suitable for large-scale production of jute and vegetables.

However, small and fragmented land-holdings coupled with lack of proper irrigation facilities happen to be the major constraint on the desired growth and productivity in the field.

Due to poor marketing facilities again, the farmers have to suffer great losses in terms of prices and surplus products to the advantage of hoarders and other outside businessmen.

There is an acute power crisis as well, and a high power transmitter is yet to be installed in the area to boost up irrigation system through increased use of power pumps.

Most of the people are landless and only alternative economic activities undertaken by them range between daily-wage-earnings and some petty businesses carried on in various hats and bazars within the subdivision and in the neighbouring Garo Hills district.

Excessive vulnerability of the area to recurring and devastating floods and consequent erosion, which counts very heavily upon the life of the people, is yet another burning problem.

Unmitigated poverty with flood ravages and consequent settlement problems on the one hand, and lack of employment opportunities on the other have compelled the people to migrate not only to other places of the subdivision and far off places like Guwahati, Dibrugarh etc. of the State, but also to cross over to the neighbouring State of Meghalaya either as labourers, job-seekers or petty businessmen.

It may be mentioned that South Salmara and Sukchar towns, both of which have existed since the past 200 years are being persistently eroded by the mighty Brahmaputra and are facing the danger of imminent extinction. A lot of people of these two towns have upon finding no way out for their rehabilitation, migrated on a large scale to the neighbouring plain areas of Hallidayganj, Phulbari, Chibinang, and Bhularbhita under Garo Hills district, mostly for permanent settlement.

While settlement of Assam's residents on a permanent basis mainly in the plains portion of the Garo Hills and alleged manipulation in issuing patta to them by the concerned GDC Mondals is viewed upon as adversely affecting the interests of the indigenous nontribal people owing to sudden upshot in land value to more than a lakh per bigha, especially in Hallidayganj, there is also a serious apprehension of this posing a really serious problem leaving enough room for future complications in terms of foreigners' influx, and consequent screening and avoidable local public harassment.

Deemed as one of the gateways to Bangladesh, as also of infiltration of Bangladeshis into India, various criminal and unlawful activities like theft, dacoity, cattle lifting, black-marketeering and many other unauthorized transactions pervade this subdivision across the border.

During the last few years, the rate of crime in the area has increased substantially, especially involving financial squabbling over an ill-gotten property, and has achieved alarming proportions in the recent past. Characteristically river-trodden and predominantly a char area tagged with acute communication bottleneck, mere police efforts to check such crimes, without identifying the modus operandi, often prove ineffective, while many an interior place still runs without even a police out post.

As various factors contribute to the commission of crimes, this also poses a threat, both internal and external, to the security of the country.

While the causes of outside threat are somehow understandable, a number of factors account for causing an internal one, and are deemed to arise, inter-alia, from prolonged neglect, economic depression and backwardness of a particular place, which incite crimes and violence, including anti-national activities, sooner or later, among different evil elements already rampant in a society.

One is aware that a large tract of Indian Territory in the Mankachar border sector is already under illegal occupation of Bangladesh. In addition, the frequent tensions, created over the erections of barbed wired fencing and constitution of a road along the border, leave much room for apprehending a threat, sooner or later.

Similarly, the border area people being, more or less, susceptible to becoming tools in the hands of foreign agencies, and if the situation in the Punjab and Kashmir is any guide, a future internal threat here also cannot be ruled out altogether unless the government, in all its wisdom considers taking up adequate economic measures, besides the necessary tight security steps, for gearing up development process in the subdivision right now itself before the time runs out.

(Published in The Shillong Times, dated February 20, 1990 By A. Islam)

o0o

Dhubri District Association On +2 Education

The two-day biennial conference of the Dhubri District HS School Teachers' & Employees' Association, held in the premises of the Janata HS School at Kharuabanda, concluded on February 6 with a call for unification of the existing three sets of institutions running the +2 stage of education in Assam and its separation from the secondary schools, as also from the degree colleges, to pave the path for establishment of fully separate and independent units of the system for improvement in the quality of education in the State.

Addressing the open session on the concluding day of the conference the Minister of State, Forests, Pension and Public Grievances, Sri Aminul Islam spoke at length on the subject amidst a large gathering of representatives of teachers and local public and agreed in principle with the call for unification and separation of +2 stage of education and assured the teachers representatives and members of the association to take up the issue with the authorities in Education department including the Minister, Education and the Chief Minister of Assam.

Taking a cue from the speeches delivered by the former Assam Assembly Speaker, Sri Giasuddin Ahmed, and the vice-president, All Assam HS Teachers' & Employees' Association, Dr. Gobinda Das, the Minister again said that there was indeed the need for review and reconsideration of the present policy on +2 stage of education by the government, and re-emphasized the contention of Dr. Das, saying that the government must not consider the expenses and probable allocation on education as 'expenditure alone but investment' which does give return in terms of human resources development in the country as a whole. He added that he would do everything possible on his part in this regard.

The Minister also called for a statewide discussion on the issue to be floated through radio, TV, newspapers and other such media and to hold seminars, etc. in order to create conditions and public opinions on it for evolving a consensus before +2 system could be separated to fit with the changes of time.

Earlier, a seminar, held on the subject, was attended, among others, by Dr. Ahijuddin Sk, Prof. Mankachar College, Shri Ashraful Ali Chief President, South Salmara-Mankachar Teachers' Coordination Committee, and Sri Anowar Islam, Advocate and President, Hatsingimari Press Club.

The Seminar was inaugurated and conducted by Prof. Abu Al Kashem of Goalpara College and Dr. Gobinda Das, vice-President, All Assam HS Teachers' & Employees' Association respectively.

Participating in the seminar, Sri Ashraful Ali lamented on the superiority and inferiority complexes including other psychological disturbances suffered by the HS teachers as direct consequences of amalgamation of +2 stage with the secondary schools. He also made a particular reference to the practice of principal or vice-principal posts being given to a mere graduate secondary teachers as against Masters' degree-holding HS teachers, causing problems of maladjustment in school administration. Dr. Ahijuddin Sk, however, was virtually sandwiched between a highly longer speeches by Prof Abu Al Kashem and Sri Ashraful Ali successively and the abrupt decision for winding up the seminar due to shortage of time as also due to arrival of the minister and the chief guest, Sri Aminul Islam for the open session that followed.

The president, Hatsingimari Press Club, Sri Anowar Islam, who was allotted only five minutes' time to complete his speech, threw somewhat a different light on the topic. Sri Islam while expressing his full agreement with the call for separation of +2 state, emphasized on the need for unification of the movement of the association into a single point on separation and unification instead of going with a bunch of issues only to crumble under it own weight.

The conference also reconstituted its executive committee with the outgoing president, Sri B.K. Deb and secretary, Sri

Aminul Islam Mondal being retained in the same capacity and posts. Thirty four more members were included in the body. The conference was followed by a cultural show in the evening of the concluding day.

Earlier, as many as eight retired HS principals, subject teachers including lower division assistants were felicited in the open session by the association.

(A Report by A. Islam published in The Assam Tribune, dated February 24,1999)

o0o

www.ingramcontent.com/pod-product-compliance
Lightning Source LLC
LaVergne TN
LVHW050416160726
843469LV00041B/1095

* 9 7 8 9 3 5 4 5 8 0 2 5 3 *